PROPHECIES OF THE DROWNED ORACLE

Stories

Robin Egberts

www.robinegberts.com

ISBN: 978-90-832686-0-6

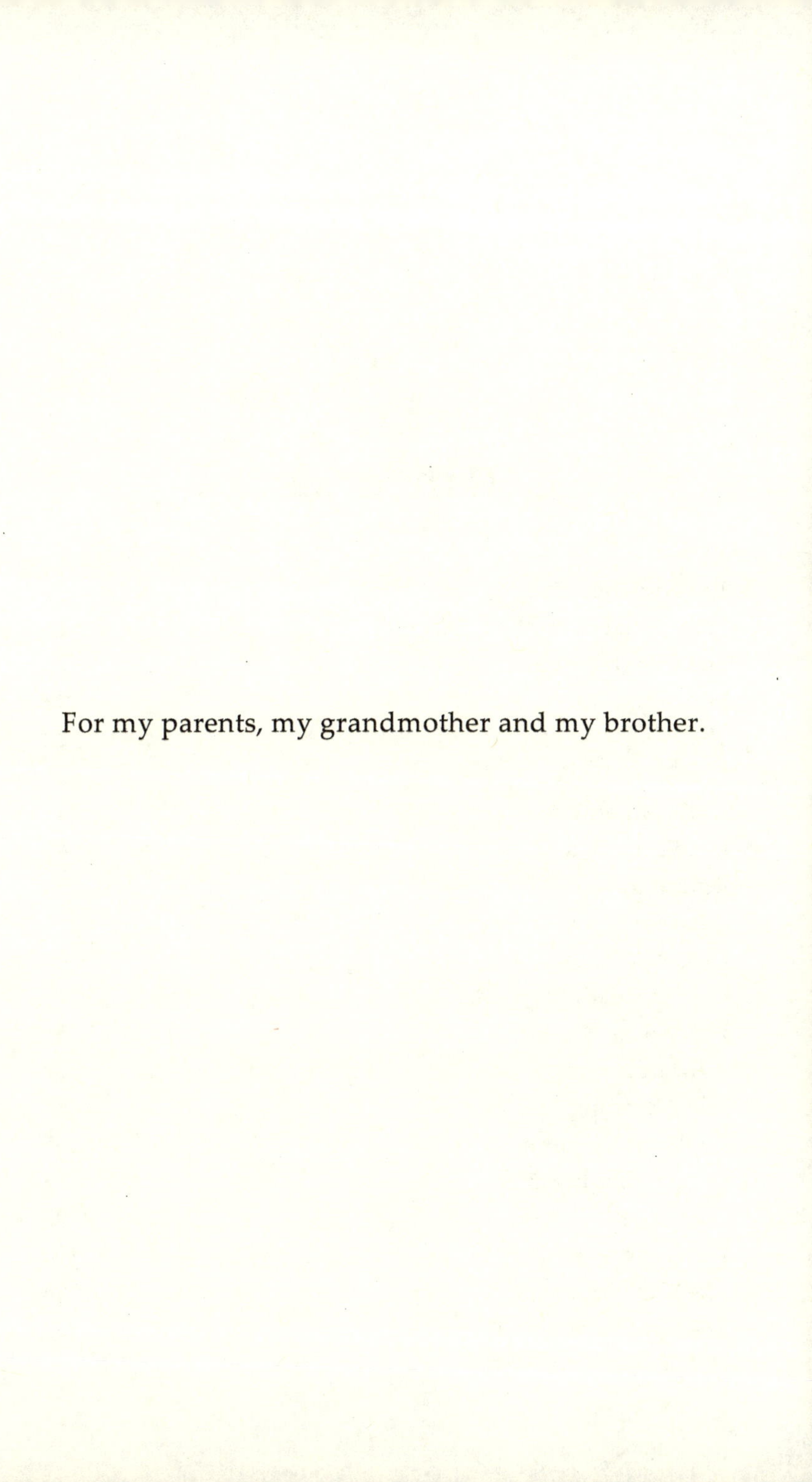

For my parents, my grandmother and my brother.

Contents

The Drowned Oracle

In the dark of the previous night, Denise pushed a man to his watery grave. So naturally, after a restful few hours of sleep, she spent the morning with the local oracle to learn if she was destined to be caught for the crime or not.

She wasn't really worried about the police, but she *was* worried about possible revenge plots. Establishing herself in the area was slow going, and while getting that man out of the way was necessary, if she were to be caught by his supporters she just didn't have the manpower to defend herself.

Denise stared at the oracle in disbelief. "Is this a joke?" The oracle stared back, emotionless as oracles tend to be.

"No." She picked up her crystal ball and carefully placed it back in its fancy purple box. "I have divined your future, you still have to pay."

" 'A different oracle knows.' " Denise said, tone mocking. She stood up, hair falling in her face as she leaned forward over the table. "You didn't give me my future you told me to take my business elsewhere!"

"No," the oracle said again. She pushed a box already filled with coins at Denise. "That was your prediction, now pay."

On the bus home, Denise tried to distract herself by reading the paper. A few pages in, her eyes were drawn to an advertisement.

'The Drowned Oracle'.

Huh. An oracle of drownings. That sounded exactly like what she needed. And the tour was that very day. How convenient. Maybe the other oracle wasn't full of shit after all.

The Drowned Oracle was, fittingly, located on a small island. The weather was nice, the sun warm. And the boat ride promised to be pleasant.

And it would have been, if it weren't for the smell.

The closer they got to the island, the worse it got. Putrid and stale. She wasn't the only one scrunching her nose when stepping off the boat.

On the pier was a sign reading 'Drowned Oracle Tour'. If she ignored the smell, the place could be called nice. The pier was a little old but not unclean. The sandy beach was lined by bushes and plants, and further down were trees in which birds sang.

In the distance she could see a grey stone building with a gravel path leading to it. Someone just exited the door. On either side of the building, a tall dike spread out, made of something that looked like black stones.

Two kids ran for the beach immediately after leaving the boat, their father storming after them. A different girl looked like she wanted to join them, but couldn't for the iron grip her mother had on her hand.

Behind Denise, the long-haired man who'd sat next to her on the boat offered to help an old lady onto the pier. The old lady scoffed. "If I needed help balancing I'd be using a cane."

The person coming from the building reached them. He cleared his throat, gathering everyone's attention. "Welcome to the Oracle's Eye. I will be your tour guide today." He had slick black hair parted in the middle. His dress was formal, with a neat white blouse and dark waistcoat. He had a calm air about him.

He looked over the group, pausing when the bald man and his two children joined them. "I would advise no children be taken along on the tour. As stated in the brochure."

Denise wondered what all was in the brochure. She only ever saw the newspaper advertisement.

The bald man scoffed, and the tall woman still clutching her daughter's hand didn't look any happier. Seeing that he wasn't getting through to them, the tour guide tried again. "The Oracle is, in simple terms, a bloated corpse. It is not suitable for young eyes."

The words 'Drowned Oracle' rearranged themselves in Denise's mind. Not an oracle of drownings, or even an oracle of the drowned... but an oracle who just happened to have drowned. One whose corpse she was apparently going to be seeing. Great.

The bald man shook his head. "Well, *I* saw the Oracle when I was ten. And I turned out just fine." Denise thought his children looked much younger than ten. One bounced around excitedly and couldn't be older than six. The words bloated corpse clearly meant nothing to him. The other, much more nervous, child was probably seven or eight. The girl shuffled on her feet and glanced back at the boat.

The guide stared the bald man down. "I really would suggest—"

"Oh, are you going to stop us from going on the tour? Slam the door in our faces?" When the guide didn't respond, the man smiled. "I *hope* we see the Oracle today. It's an important character-building experience."

It's then that another person joined them, having walked down the gravel path unnoticed while everyone was occupied. "I couldn't agree more," the person said. They were of the ambiguously gendered trenchcoat-wearing type. Similarly formal to the tour guide, but with a little more wear and tear in the fabric. "You know, the city council won't allow children to live here on the Eye, but I say—"

"Well, I definitely don't want my daughter to see something that will give her nightmares," the tall woman interrupted. "Surely you can control the thing to stay out of sight while we take the tour?" Still holding her mother's hand, the girl glanced from the guide to her mother. She indeed didn't seem too thrilled at the prospect of seeing a corpse.

The new person zeroed in on the tall woman, gaze blazing. Denise watched with interest.

The tour guide stepped between the new person and the tall woman before anything could be said. Denise couldn't help but feel disappointed. "No," the guide said. Which should have been obvious since they were talking about a corpse. If they could control it then the tour would be a lot more popular. You don't see a proper necromancy show every day.

The tall woman scowled. "So you would have my daughter see something like that? She's thirteen!"

The tour guide rolled his eyes. "No, I would have you remove your daughter from the situation."

The woman looked ready to continue complaining until she got her way, but the guide's stony expression must have communicated his finality. "Fine," she said. She turned, pulling her daughter along as she stormed back to the boat. "But you won't see me paying for a tour I didn't go on!"

The tour guide sighed and the group was silent for an awkward moment. Denise wondered if she should leave as well. She wasn't all that hot on viewing random corpses, and since she wouldn't be getting her promised prophecy there wasn't much point in staying. But on the other hand, she was kind of curious why there was a corpse viewing with tour attached on this island.

Meanwhile, the older of the two remaining children tried to slip away to the boat, but her father grabbed her shoulder and gave her a stern glare. Other than her, none of the other tour goers indicated they wanted to follow the tall woman and her daughter.

The new person smiled and clapped their hands, drawing everyone's attention. "I am one of the Oracle's valued disciples. I will be accompanying the tour to clear up any confusion or…" they glanced at the tour guide with poorly masked venom, "misrepresentations."

"Right," the tour guide said with an admirably blank face after the clear insult. "Since the island is shared by worshippers and researchers alike, we share the tour as well." His tone made clear how very thrilled he was about that. "Let's head to our first destination, shall we?"

The guide led them along the gravel path. "The island isn't natural. It was created by people long ago."

The youngest child gasped in delight. He grabbed his sister's hand and swung it wildly. "How did they do that?" he asked.

While the tour guide explained, Denise looked around, a little surprised. Though, with how old the island was, she supposed most visible evidence of how humans created it was covered up by nature by now. The shape was a little odd.

As they got closer to the building and the dike looming on either side of it, the grass next to the path grew yellow and brittle, until eventually there wasn't any grass left. There weren't any trees in the centre of the island either.

"This building is the centre of activity of the Oracle's Eye," the guide said as he opened the door. The group followed him into the building. "Here we do research into the Oracle and the various mysteries surrounding it."

"Her," the disciple said. "The mysteries surrounding her."

The guide and worshipper stood at the front of the group, behind them was a wall with two windows through which she could see water. "Unless the Oracle professes a preference for pronoun use, I'll just assume it's fine with any." The disciple went to interrupt, but the guide continued in a musing tone. "Or has it shown itself to you more than others?"

The disciple sent the guide a thunderous glare, to which he only looked smug.

Denise wondered if she misinterpreted the meaning of Drowned Oracle again. Was it a bloated corpse or was it something capable of having pronoun preferences? Suddenly the tall woman's demand to control the Oracle made a little more sense.

"Anyways, the research building has three levels. This one, which contains the hallway and gift shop. Downstairs, which is below water level and which we'll visit shortly. And upstairs, which contains the sleeping quarters for the researchers. We won't be visiting them for privacy reasons, though they go largely unused anyway."

"If they're still as mouldy as they used to be, then I don't blame them," the old lady said.

"You're familiar?" the tour guide asked.

"I used to work here," the old lady said. "That was before we were allowed to sleep away from the island. You can imagine why I left." She glanced at the disciple.

The disciple gave her a disdainful look. "As you can see, not everyone can be chosen by the Oracle."

"The Oracle doesn't choose anyone," the tour guide said with a long-suffering tone. "But as you can see, the disciples of the Oracle were once researchers as well. They just..."

"Never left?" the old lady said.

"Right."

The long-haired man leaned into Denise's space to whisper, "Went mad at the sight of it, no doubt." She didn't appreciate the closeness. Luckily he moved away again after his comment. From the way the disciple talked, Denise had to agree with him.

The old lady snorted, causing the long-haired man to colour in embarrassment at having been heard. "If the sight of the Oracle didn't do it then it was the dreams."

"Dreams?" Denise asked.

"Yeah the Oracle—"

The old lady was interrupted by the tour guide clearing his throat. "We have limited time here, ladies." He took a step back and gestured at the window.

"Here out the window, you can see the waters in which the Drowned Oracle resides. We'll be getting a closer look at it and the dike surrounding it later. It is perfectly round, and a whole kilometre across. We suspect it was built for research purposes, but we don't know for sure."

The disciple smiled. "Any questions?" Then, before anyone could answer, they clapped their hands. "Great! Let's move on."

The tour guide opened a door on the wall to the left of the group and motioned them in. Denise filed in as one of the last, only the long-haired man behind her. They descended a set of metal stairs. One of those with holes in it to make them less slippery.

Descending the stairs felt a little like going underwater. The air was colder and felt damp. There hung a mustiness in the space not unlike mould. It probably *was* mould. The stones in the room they entered were stained like the water had soaked through them.

The space was cramped, even for the small group, but they managed. The two guides were once again at the front of the group. The children were positioned so they could see, with the adults behind them.

The long-haired man, who stood next to Denise, muttered he was getting a headache. No wonder in this space.

The guides stood on either side of a big window looking out into the lake. Or it would have, if the water wasn't so murky. "The view would be spectacular if the water was clear," the disciple said, "Sorry about that."

That's a shame. Denise kind of wanted to see the Oracle now and see what all the fuss was about. "Unlucky for us."

The tour guide sighed. "It's always like this. If it isn't a bacteria bloom then it's algae."

The other side of the glass showed only a green haze. Some people leaned forward in hopes of seeing something, including the smallest child. But there was nothing.

As the tour guide continued talking, Denise lost interest, but not everyone had the same idea. The elder of the children screamed, pointing at the window. Everyone looked to see a sizeable shadow. For a moment, Denise thought it was a limb. Was she going to see the Oracle after all? But no, the shadow moved, slinking, the movement betraying it as a large fish.

There were multiple sighs of relief around the room. The bald man quietly reprimanded his kid for being dramatic, but in the quiet space, everyone could hear.

"Are there many fish in the lake?" The long-haired man asked to dispel the awkward atmosphere. It was a good question, distracting Denise from watching the bald man and his daughter. While a smell like that didn't *have* to indicate poor water quality, it would at the very least indicate an oxygen problem.

"More than you'd expect, given the anaerobic conditions." The tour guide chuckled awkwardly. "The Oracle eats them, we think." He fell silent. He glanced at the disciple. "What? No comment?"

The disciple rolled their eyes. "Unlike some, I don't delude myself in thinking our magnificent Oracle is somehow above eating animal products."

The tour guide shrugged. "Fair enough."

While the two guides had a moment of unity, Denise registered an odd sound behind her. A clacking as if someone was typing on a keyboard. Turning, she noticed the sound came from behind a solid metal door. The tour guide noticed her shift in attention.

"Ah, that there is the room where the researchers compile their data and the scribes work to translate the Oracle's prophecies," the guide explained, gaze intense. Denise instantly paid more attention.

The disciple stepped forward, hands clasped eagerly. "The Oracle, when she's deep under water, sings in a tone too low for human ears to hear. Though some people may feel it in their bodies," they said with a shiver. "For those of us who live here, it may cause marvellous dreams—"

"Can it cause headaches?" the long-haired man asked, interrupting the disciple.

The disciple pursed their lips and took in the pained scrunch of the man's brow. Their expression grew more severe by the second. They didn't otherwise respond.

The tour guide stepped in when the disciple kept silent. "Yes, it can."

"If the Oracle disapproves of you," the disciple said in a low tone.

The tour guide looked very much like he wanted to punch his counterpart. "Or just because some people are more sensitive to the low-frequency tones."

Denise was getting irritated at this continued waffling. "What is this about prophecies?" It was increasingly likely she was in the right place after all.

The tour guide stared at her for a moment. "Right." He straightened back up into the pose she was starting to recognise as the one he used when reciting practised lines. "Now, the Oracle is most known for coming to the surface periodically and imparting the names of the drowned. These names, whispered to whoever happens to be near, are always accurate, and part of the duties of those on the island is to record these names and inform the families of the departed. What you might not know, is that when the Oracle isn't imparting names, it sings. We have equipment that can record the low frequencies of its song. We have one here." He pushed through the group to a corner of the room. The group rearranged so they could all see.

While shuffling around, Denise bumped into the long-haired man. His expression had grown more strained, and it appeared he hadn't noticed they were moving around at all. He whispered an apology and moved in the proper direction. Denise followed, ending up close to the door where she could hear the clacking sound even more clearly. The old lady, noticing the interaction, leaned closer and whispered, "It's not just the song that induces headaches. Some people react more strongly to the radiation—"

The tour guide cleared his throat. "This machine here detects the low frequencies of the Oracle's song and records them on this line here." He pointed to a roll of paper coming out of the machine. As they watched, it continued to unroll further. A bit of graphite moved back and forth over the paper, creating a jagged line not unlike a heart monitor. "Our scribes have learned to decipher the machines' output into words."

"That's where the prophecies come in," the disciple interrupted. "Some of what the Oracle prophesies has already come to pass. Others happen at the very moment she sings it. And the most magnificent are those that have yet to happen."

The tour guide continued. "Some songs appear to be about other worlds entirely. There is some debate as to whether these are the Oracle creating fictional stories for its entertainment, or if these other worlds really exist."

"Well," said the disciple. "*I* think our world will at some point change so much that those prophecies will come true as well. There is no need, and no evidence, to think other worlds exist."

Out of the disciple's sight, the tour guide rolled his eyes.

There was a lull in the clacking sound behind the door. Denise listened closer, only to jump away at the sound of a loud cackle. It sounded deranged. Something flashed in the tour guide's eyes.

There was a moment of silence as the group stared at the door before the clacking picked up again. "Our magnificent Oracle can be very funny at times," the disciple said blandly.

As the tour guide rambled about visiting the gift shop next, Denise's mind wandered. Prophecies. It was a different kind of future sight than that of the oracle she'd visited earlier that day. Much more temperamental, and seldom anything came out of them. It did not bode anything good for her hopes of getting away with murder.

"Is there a repository for the Oracle's prophecies?" Denise asked.

The tour guide fell silent. She hadn't meant to interrupt him. Whoops. "No."

"Actually, there is," the disciple said, "It is not accessible to the public. With how dangerous prophecies can be, only a select few should be trusted with them. Like us worshippers, who have vowed to keep them safe and away from prying eyes."

"Except for the ones available in the gift shop," the tour guide said.

The disciple nodded. "Except for those."

The gift shop prophecies didn't give Denise much hope. If they were concerned about the dangers of prophecies, then it was unlikely any pertaining to her current or future situation were among them. Her gaze caught on the machine still scratching out the song currently being sung in the depths of the waters beyond the walls. Surely she could decipher it with enough time? It made sense for the needed prophecy to be made right as she was there, didn't it?

If only she could get a moment alone with it, it wouldn't be difficult to snatch the paper and stuff it in her pocket.

As the group followed the disciple up the stairs, Denise attempted to linger behind, but as the room emptied, the tour guide remained, leaning on the wall next to the door. His eyes were shadowed as he looked at her. "Are you coming?" he asked. She made sure to hide her irritation and nodded, preceding the guide up the stairs.

She settled in at the back of the group, hoping she might slip away at some point unnoticed. Though with such a small group, that was unlikely. Over the shoulders of the old lady and the bald man, she could see the rest of the room.

"This is our gift shop," the tour guide said, settling at the front of the group. Denise thought calling it a gift shop was rather generous. It was a blank room with unpainted grey stone walls and floors. The only thing in it was a bland wooden table. On it lay two stacks of books, with between them a jar, presumably for payment. The room was, in one word, bare.

The disciple lifted a book off one of the stacks, holding it up for the group to see. "This book here contains a selection of the Oracle's prophecies." Their eyes shone with fervour, and they were not alone in their excitement. The tour guide was smiling.

"I chose my favourites," he said, "it has both past and future events detailed."

But not everyone was excited. The smallest kid yawned. "Does it have pictures?" he asked.

"Not this one," The disciple said. They glanced around the room, eyes lingering on Denise for a moment. "But the other book contains photographs of the Oracle's Eye, the surrounding waters, and of course the lake in which the Oracle resides. The pictures were taken on a rare day without a bacteria or algae bloom, so they're clear as can be. And if the prospect of seeing the Oracle's home doesn't excite you, part of the profits go to the families of the divers who took the pictures."

The bald man put his hand on the shoulder of his youngest, preventing him from grabbing a copy of the book. "What happened to them?" he asked.

The disciple clutched the prophecy book to their chest. The feverish light in their eyes grew brighter as tears welled in their eyes. "The Oracle asked them to join her permanently," they whispered with emotion.

Denise grimaced. Some others in the group shuffled awkwardly. "I doubt the divers were happy about that," she muttered.

The long-haired man laughed, then winced.

The tour guide cleared his throat. "We have to continue now but you can pick up the books when we pass by here again later."

The disciple nodded frantically. "Let us move outside." Their voice trembled with excitement, and they bustled out ahead of the group.

The group filed out the door after the disciple. Denise hung back, hoping to go unnoticed. But she wasn't the only one. The older child lingered in the doorway, expression fearful. Her father noticed though and pushed her along. As for Denise, just like before, the tour guide kept too good of an eye on her for her to slip away.

They exited the building on the other side. Instead of the ground of the island, they stood on a pier overlooking the round lake. The smell of the water hit her the moment she left the door. Next to her, the long-haired man breathed deeply, apparently unbothered by the smell. Unlike when they started, there was no more sun shining on the water. Grey clouds covered the sky. She hoped it wasn't going to rain.

"As I mentioned before, the lake is a kilometre across. The water is around 11 meters deep, and has slowly been getting deeper through the years we've been researching it."

"Don't lakes usually get shallower over time?" Denise asked.

The guide nodded. "They do."

There was a moment of silence in which she waited for him to elaborate. He didn't. "Why doesn't this one?" she asked.

"We don't know."

"Looks like there's a lot they don't know," the long-haired man joked. His face had lost the pinched expression. His headache must have gone away. "Considering they've been here for a century."

"Closer to eighty years, really," the old lady said. Though that didn't sound much better.

The tour guide cleared his throat. He gestured for them to follow. They walked a bit along the pier, which curved around the inner edge of the water for some fifty meters or so. This close to the dike, Denise noticed the odd shape of the rocks it was made out of. Lumpy and irregular, but smooth like molten metal in spots. While they were mostly black, there was a layer of oxidation on them. She wondered if the oxidation was toxic. That would explain the circle of dead plants around it that she spotted earlier.

The disciple pointed up at a part of the dike a little further away. "We disciples of the Oracle live close to the Oracle, here on the barrier of her domain. We have spread out our houses so wherever the Oracle may show up, someone will always hear." On the dike stood a couple dozen huts, spaced out regularly.

"How many of you are there?" Denise asked. The houses were dark, and she didn't see anyone else outside.

"Plenty," they said. "Though we wouldn't say no to new recruits." He glanced at the bald man.

Denise concluded they were short-staffed.

"The first of these houses were built years ago, when part

of one of the first research teams saw the light of the Oracle and never wanted to leave her side again."

Denise found herself close to the edge. She looked down at the water. An aquatic plant caught on a support beam of the pier. It was blackened with rot, except for where mould coloured it white.

"As for the dike itself," the tour guide said, "it goes all the way around the water, the research building excepted. It's ten meters high. It is made from various materials, but mostly molten metal remnants.

"We still have a select few photographs, showing how the island looked years before we researchers arrived. At one point, the dike was covered in plants. It was pretty. But something must have happened before we got here."

The old lady coughed. "That's why they sent a research team here in the first place."

"Right. We still don't know what happened, but we presume it's the same thing that killed all the plants in the water, causing the lack of oxygen. It's never really recovered from whatever event that was. Even when we tried introducing plants ourselves."

"But the Oracle likes it this way," the disciple said as some sort of reassurance.

The smallest child bounced up and down, his hand in the air. It was only his father's hand on his shoulder preventing him from bouncing right off the pier. "What if the water boiled! That would kill all the plants!" he said once the tour guide gestured for him to speak.

The tour guide groaned, but the disciple grinned. "Actually, there's a group of us who think exactly that!"

The old lady shared a commiserating look with the tour guide. "And I thought that theory would have died out by now. I still think it's something to do with the radiation. Any progress on that?"

The tour guide shuffled uncomfortably. "Nothing we're

allowed to share with the general populace."

"Fun news then," the old lady said cheerfully.

It was then that a scream drew their attention. It was the older child. She was with her brother and father, a little ways away from the group where the disciple was still extolling about their boiling water theory. She clutched her father's hand, her other arm pointed at the water.

Denise followed her gaze and saw the water roiling, and whatever was causing it was getting closer. Her heart rate shot up. The touring group unconsciously drew closer together, further away from the water's edge, but not the disciple. They stepped forward, expression rapturous. They stood so close to the edge their toes floated free above the water. They spread out their arms. "It's the Oracle!" they called, voice projected over the water, "She's blessed us with her presence!"

The roiling settled before the disciple. A shadow could be seen under the water. Then something rose, pushed up through the water, and broke the surface. The Oracle's face was worse than she imagined. It was bald, the skin on its head patchy and hanging off in strips. Its ears were eaten down to cartilage and nothing was left of its eyes, just empty, watery sockets. It opened its mouth, and in the low light of the overcast sky, Denise could see an orange phosphorescence shine through rotten teeth.

The children screamed, the nervous one with all her fears confirmed and the excited one not so excited anymore. Their father stood between them, looking catatonic. Eyes blank and lips pulled into an emotionless smile. The youngest child tried to grab his attention by shaking his hand, but it didn't work. The older child pulled her brother away and closer to the main group. The old lady, though most of her attention was focused on the Oracle as well, had enough clarity of mind to allow the children to hide their faces in her skirt.

Then the Oracle spoke. In a horrible, burbling voice, low

and pulsing. It could be felt more than heard, like the vibrations of a large engine. Names that meant nothing to Denise were listed without emotion, without pause. The older child whimpered, frantically trying to block out the sound with her hands over her ears. The old lady's face twisted and her hands shook. The tour guide spotted it and quickly pulled a notebook and pencil from his pocket. The old lady snatched them from his hands and frantically began to scribble the names.

Denise had nearly zoned out of the names themselves, hearing them without registering the sounds as words, but then one name had her breath stutter. It was him, of course it was, she should have realised. The man she pushed to his death last night. At least she knew for sure he perished. She never saw the body.

To her horror, she wasn't the only one to react to the name. The long-haired man gasped, face paling even further. He put a hand on his mouth and looked about ready to topple over. Denise steadied him before he collapsed. She just hoped her own reaction was masked by everything else.

"Someone you know?" she asked. It was insensitive, but she had to know.

"Yeah," he gasped out, "My… my friend." Denise winced. Just her luck that one of that man's groupies happened to be on the same tour. She looked around, wanting to escape the situation. In her looking, she spotted the building. The building where that machine was still holding the prophecy she needed. The building that was currently empty, or at least that room was.

She carefully lowered the man to sit. Then she pushed the tour guide in his direction. Surely he'd encountered this kind of shock before, he could deal with it. The tour guide glared at her with more venom than the action deserved, but ultimately did comfort the long-haired man.

With the Oracle still droning out names and everyone

occupied, Denise slipped away, back into the building.

Without the wind, the crying, and the droning inhuman voice, the room felt utterly silent. For a moment she stood there, hand on her chest, taking just a moment to calm herself down. She took a deep breath as her heart slowed, then moved to the top of the stairs. She listened carefully, but didn't hear anyone in the room below.

She crept down the stairs. She tried to keep her footsteps light, to remain unheard even if someone was in the room after all, but the metal stairs made that very difficult. Not only did her shoes clunk on the metal, it was also old and rusty where it met the damp stone wall. It creaked under her weight. Every step sent her heart racing, but she reached the end unnoticed.

The machine was still, but behind the other door the clacking continued. She hoped this meant the Oracle was still distracting the rest of the group. She swiftly moved to the machine and grabbed the paper. She winced as she pulled and the paper ripped with an uncomfortably loud sound. She quickly ripped it all the way, if someone heard her, it was done already, if they hadn't yet, she was better off making the sound as short as possible.

The paper tried to curl back into a roll, but she couldn't exactly carry that around unnoticed. Instead she forced it somewhat flat and folded it a few times. She didn't hear a sound from the other room. Good.

She sped up the stairs, remaining as quiet as possible. At the top she paused just long enough to check that no one was there, but she didn't hear anything. She quickly exited the door and closed it behind her.

The stink of the lake wafted through the door which must have blown open while she was downstairs. She could hear the voices of the rest of the group, still at a distance, though she didn't think she could rejoin them now unnoticed.

The folded paper crinkled in her hand. Her eyes fell on

the stack of books. That should be a good excuse.

She grabbed a prophecy book from the stack and stuffed the stolen prophecy inside somewhere in the middle. She breathed a sigh of relief. She wasn't caught. Happy with herself, she put a bit more money than necessary in the payment jar.

She walked to the side of the table and leaned against the wall, opening the book to leaf through it while waiting for the others to join her.

She just heard footsteps nearing the door when something caught her eye. Her name. She flipped to the start of the story, skimming the whole thing frantically, ignoring whoever just stepped inside.

It was all there. Everything written down. From her arrival on the island to this very moment. She looked up, straight into the eyes of the tour guide, who looked at her with all the venom of someone who knew she was a murderer.

A fake smile twitched his lips. "I understand. The Oracle can be... overwhelming."

Denise swallowed. "Right."

The rest of the group filed in. The old lady went first, looking haunted, shoving the notebook and pen at the tour guide and fleeing back out in the direction of the boat. The children followed. After them, their father, still catatonic, was pushed along by the smiling disciple.

And last, was the long-haired man. His grief seemed short-lived, his face now twisted in a mask of anger. Thankfully not yet directed at her. She knew that wouldn't last long, as she watched the tour guide hand him a copy of the prophecy book. "On the house, for your loss," he said with a smug smile in Denise's direction.

Denise trudged the path to the boat as if in a daze. The tour guide didn't ask for the prophecy back as he waved them off at the pier. And Denise wasn't about to offer it to him. Though she doubted it would give her any important information. She'd already read the prophecy regarding her, after all. She could easily figure out the rest herself.

Soon, the long-haired man would read the book and realise who murdered his boss, and then he'd come after her.

As they boarded the boat, the tall woman and her daughter took one look at the despondent expressions and pale faces before looking very relieved they skipped out on the tour.

She pressed her face in her hands as she sat down, as far away from the long-haired man as the small vessel allowed. 'A different oracle knows' indeed.

She looked up, gaze resting on the man in question as he settled down himself.

His new book open in his lap.

She better decide which side of the boat was best to jump from in advance.

Toad Expanse and Dune Grass

Grace triumphantly steps onto the gravel path. She's finally found it, after all those years she's finally found Toad Expanse; A hidden clearing in a dune forest. The road to it was blocked off by plants and debris. But now she's here, and it's beautiful.

Prickly grey-green bushes clutter the sandy ground. Leftovers of what once were proper paths criss-cross the enormous clearing at different levels and are lined with dune grass. Where Grace stands, the road that led her here splits into two. Partly hidden behind a bush, between the two paths, stands a short wooden post with a still vibrant red arrow on it pointing to the right. It would probably lead to the middle of the clearing.

Grace would like to explore, but she's very warm. The sun brings an oppressive heat to the clearing, but the light itself is oddly cold. It's the light of a dark cloudy day, but brighter, and when Grace looks up, the sky is blue. There are no discernible shadows anywhere in sight. Grace pauses and wrinkles her brow. With effort, her sluggish mind begins to work a little. She looks at her watch; Three O'clock. She looks away. Now some of the bushes cast light shadows on the sandy ground. She looks back at her watch; Seven O'clock.

A grin spreads on her face, her mind clears. This is a dream.

She takes a moment to consider her surroundings. What had she called this place earlier? Toad Expanse? What does that even mean? Okay, whatever, it doesn't matter. Now that she's lucid, she can do what she has to do: think of Emma.

Not a second after the thought enters her mind, Grace hears footsteps behind her. She turns around and there she is, Emma, standing right there on the gravel path, wearing her favourite pastel purple shirt over light blue jeans. "It worked," Grace breathes.

"It worked!" Emma screams. She jumps up and down and embraces Grace. Grace feels Emma's weight pressing against her. Even though this is just a dream, she can really feel Emma. Emma lets go and bounces a little on her toes. "You really did it! Now we can still see each other even when I'm gone."

Grace smiles. "I'm just glad I managed it in time." She takes in the sight of Emma a little longer, just taking in her presence, that she's really there. She turns towards the path with the arrow. She's familiar by now with the mechanics of dreams and knows exactly how reliable paths really are. This one, which turns to the left after a few metres, completely obscuring the rest from sight, is perfect for a change of scenery.

She gestures for Emma to follow. The moment they take the turn, Emma gasps. The tall trees surrounding the clearing have fallen away. The criss-crossing paths are gone. The only thing left is the grass. Roiling dunes covered in grass as far as the eye can see. Emma steps forward to get a better look. Grace just watches her. She sits down on the grass and watches Emma take in the view. The wind catches Emma's hair, brushing her short brown locks over her face, and then continues over the dunes, making waves in the grass.

After a while, Emma joins Grace. Unlike actual dune grass, which is hard and sharp enough to cut into your skin if you aren't careful, the grass here is soft. They sit there for a while in silence, happy to just be together.

"I've never had a lucid dream before," Emma says, breaking the silence.

"You still haven't," says Grace. At Emma's confused look, she continues. "This isn't the same thing as a normal lucid dream. Those are in your own mind, but right now... well, instead of being in your mind or my mind, we're somewhere in between." Grace leans her chin on her knees. "I'm not sure exactly how it works."

"Magic, I guess," Emma says.

"Yeah." Grace sighs and flops onto her back. She stares up at the empty blue sky.

She hears a faint shuffling next to her as Emma lies down as well. "Was it that last chapter that you were having trouble with, or was it something else?"

Grace groans. "Both," she says. The book about dream magic was complicated. Too complicated. Written for witches far more skilled than her. Really, would it have killed the author to use simpler language? She throws an arm over her face. "I missed a link between the last chapter and chapter 5. I couldn't just follow the ritual instructions word for word, they had to be personalised."

"How were you supposed to do that?"

"To be honest, I'm still not sure." She huffs and turns her head. She can just see Emma from under her arm. "I just knew I wouldn't be able to do it in time, so I took a shortcut."

Emma touches her shoulder. "You still have three weeks," she murmurs.

"That wasn't enough." Grace shakes her head. "I do wonder if it was the best idea..."

"What was the shortcut?" Emma sounds worried.

"I just... let my subconscious do the work. Instead of

filling in all the details of the ritual I just let them fill themselves out."

"Like a dream," Emma breathes.

"Exactly."

"But not a lucid dream," Emma says, still working through the logic in her mind. Her brows are furrowed deep in thought, or maybe it's worry, Grace isn't sure.

"No, not a lucid dream." Grace lets her arm slip from her face. There are clouds now. Neither of them put them there.

"Isn't that dangerous?"

High above, two cloud armies prepare for war as their respective clouds drift nearer. "Only as dangerous as any normal dream."

"A normal dream with magic involved, you mean," Emma says pointedly.

"Ah— yeah. But it seems to have worked well enough. I don't think anything will go wrong now."

"Famous last words," Emma says.

Grace turns to the side, her face turned towards Emma. Emma does the same. They're close like this. Their knees brush together where they've pulled up their legs. Grace tries to sound reassuring as she says, "The only thing that can go wrong now, from what I know, is that this all turns out to just have been a regular dream. You aren't real, and when I ask tomorrow you'll have no idea what I'm talking about."

Emma doesn't look at her, eyes instead glued to the grass between them. Grace takes the moment to examine the light freckles scattered over her cheeks and nose. "And it could be the same for me," says Emma as she absentmindedly picks a flower out of the grass that didn't have any flowers before this. Grace watches her twirl the thin stem between elegant fingers. "We should think of a way to confirm with each other that this was real."

Grace looks up into Emma's eyes. They shine golden in the sunlight lighting up her face. "Like an impossible question?"

"Yes." Emma smiles. She reaches out the hand holding the flower and gently pushes it behind Grace's ear. Emma's hand is warm where it brushes the side of her face. "Something impossible to guess that would 100% confirm that we met tonight."

That morning, Grace wakes up feeling excited. She almost pulls the extension chord off her nightstand when she forgets to pull out her phone charger. Irritated, she yanks the chord out and pulls her phone towards her. She squints her eyes at the bright screen as she navigates to her contacts. She stares at Emma's name for a moment, then swipes over her screen before she can change her mind.

A low beep against her ear, another one. Grace nervously moves her legs under her blanket. What if it wasn't real and Emma thinks she's crazy? Another beep. Grace closes her eyes and takes a deep breath. It'll be fine, it will be fine. Emma has never thought she was weird before, this is nothing compared to everything else. It will be—

Her thought is broken by a crackle on the other end, followed by a sleepy "Hello?". Grace swallows. The words are stuck in her throat. "Grace?"

At the sound of her name, spoken in Emma's sleep heavy voice, something within Grace settles. The words slip out without a thought. "The dune grass waves to you."

A second of silence. Grace almost begins to panic again, but then Emma answers, "The cloud-dwellers wave back."

The Cloud Dwellers

I lie on a soft patch of grass. The wind rustles the leaves of the trees I can see around the edges of my vision. The calming sound is accompanied by the singing of birds, and far off somewhere in the distance, I can hear a wild boar mulling around. Footsteps sound on the gravel path behind me. I'm only barely hidden behind a small bush, they could easily see me, but they don't. The girls are far too absorbed in each other to notice. The voices drift away as they walk further down the path until the only thing that's left is a soft unintelligible murmur.

I watch the clouds above me drift slowly across the sky. Nothing could be better than this view. Nothing can turn me away from this spectacle. In the clouds, I see people. I see knights in armour, horses galloping and bucking; a battle. The swords clash against each other, but the sound doesn't reach me. They're too far above, but I can imagine.

The screams of wounded soldiers, the fearful whinnying of their horses, the rumble of a thousand hooves hitting the ground in frantic patterns. A sword breaks under the weight of a horse's leg. It stomps down in a panic as an enemy soldier swipes at its rider. Another attack, another dodge. Heavy legs nearly crush a motionless hand, still loosely grasping onto the reigns of an equally still horse. Their still forms a morbid oasis in the midst of a raging storm. A violent whirlwind that struck them down ruthlessly, yet—mercifully—together.

Theirs was a deep bond, I can tell. They must have met when they were young. I can easily see it. Born on the same day of the same year. The boy's father handing him the reigns and telling him, "If you take good care of him, he'll do the same for you." The boy looking into the horse's big cloudy eyes and knowing he's made a friend for life.

They grow up together. They ride through the cloudy forests, bathe in rivers of mist, eat white berries that are said to grant clairvoyance to the lucky, all before—always—returning home where father would be waiting for them with warm food and a soft bed. On days when night falls before they returned from yet another journey, the boy curls up against his companion's side. A place so warm and comfortable he doesn't need a fire to stave off the cold.

They know the cloudlands better than even most merchants, and use their knowledge to guide lost travellers and bring messages to and from distant towns and cities. Back home, father listens to his son's stories with a small smile.

But then came the war.

I watch them from below. Two clouds crashing together to become one, but first fighting a desperate battle. Two armies made of soldiers all dragged from their peaceful lives on the whims of nature. Two figures, lying motionless between their still fighting comrades, gone on a journey they will never return from.

I can't hear their swords clash, but I can imagine.

Mushroom

Around the edge of the garden, something moved. The bushes rustled. Whatever it was made a chirping sound unlike any bird Megan knew. Something small and brown moved between the leaves. She sat up and tried to get a better look. Was it a mouse? It moved out of the bushes. Her heart froze.

A mushroom.

The thing waddled over the grass. Its brown cap shone in the sunlight. It swayed a little on its pale stem as it moved. Megan jumped up. Wand drawn in a shaky hand, she came at the creature. From this close, she could see its hyphae coming out from under its cap. Pale, as thin as human hair. Floating in the wind like tentacles, feeling, sensing. Its stem was no thicker than her wrist, the cap about the size of a small dessert plate. Some hyphae carefully examined the ground, the grass, settled on a dandelion. It didn't have eyes, but the undulating hyphae seemed to study her with the same childish curiosity as it examined the flower.

Megan faltered, she lowered her wand. It was, dare she say it, cute.

But mushrooms weren't cute. They were dangerous. Creatures of death, of decay. Evil and filled with the darkest magic.

It seemed to deem her unthreatening, for it waddled a little closer. Megan stepped back before any of its hyphae could touch her. No way was she letting it taint her with its darkness. The hyphae that it had stretched out towards her leg drooped. She couldn't help but smile. It really was cute...

She glanced at the wand in her hand. She knew what she was supposed to do. Kill it before it tainted her garden further than it already had. But as she glanced back at the creature so delightfully examining a dandelion like it was the most precious thing in the world... Maybe she'd watch it for a little longer.

Megan sat in her favourite shady spot, under an old birch tree in the centre of her garden. And watched the little mushroom waddle around. She still held her wand, ready to use it at the first sign of trouble, but for the moment it was unnecessary.

The mushroom had moved on from the dandelion and now sat in the middle of a group of daisies. Its hyphae drifted gently in the wind, occasionally brushing one of the flowers. Every time they did, the mushroom chirped happily.

Thus far, it had done none of the evil things Megan had been warned against. It hadn't spread any spores around. It hadn't summoned a whole army of fellow mushrooms. It hadn't tried to constrict her in its hyphae to grow its children in her corpse. The plants it touched hadn't died. Not even the dragonfly that landed on its cap seemed to get harmed in any way. The mushroom made a chortling sound when it happened, apparently delighted a dragonfly would choose its cap to perch on. It waved its hyphae like a human would their hand as the dragonfly left.

Megan wondered if she'd encountered the one *not* evil mushroom, or if all of them were like this. Maybe this one was evil as well, and she'd been fooled by its harmless appearance. She shook her head, she couldn't imagine this cute creature had done a single bad thing in its life.

As she refocused on the mushroom, she found it a lot closer to her than she remembered. It waddled towards her, hyphae outstretched like the arms of a toddler wanting to be picked up. Megan didn't move away this time. It hadn't hurt the dragonfly, so it wouldn't hurt her either.

When it reached her foot, it stopped. It gently tapped her shoe with its hyphae before curling one around it. It toddled closer, still wrapped around her foot. It examined her leg like this until it was close enough for Megan to reach out. In the shadows under the tree, its cap had a subtle purple tint.

Megan didn't know where the compulsion came from, but she wanted to pet it. She reached out her hand. A few hair-like hyphae brushed against her skin. They tickled but didn't hurt or even itch, as she'd still somewhat expected from the stories she'd heard. Its cap felt soft and smooth. Silky. It was cool to the touch. When Megan petted it like she would her cat, it made a pleased chirping noise that transformed into a high pitched purr as she continued.

It really was adorable.

More hyphae came out from under the cap. How did they all fit under there? They curled around her hand, her arm. They examined the hand still resting on the ground and entwined with her fingers. They touched her face, tapped all her features. Megan closed her eyes and allowed them to tap over her eyelids.

Her nose tingled. She sneezed. The mushroom twitched under her hand and pulled back from her face. Megan laughed. "I didn't mean to startle you, I just got some dust in my nose."

The mushroom chirped. Megan got the sense that it was happy.

The tingle in her nose didn't go away. She sneezed again. The mushroom chirped softly. It touched her face, squeezed the hyphae entwined with her fingers in reassurance. A warm happiness quieted her mind. Megan watched the hyphae float around. In the darkening shadow of the tree, the pale hyphae seemed to glow a near orange. She strained her eyes, her vision was fuzzy.

She yawned. It was like the mushroom itself was radiating warmth and light. Light the colour of liquid honey, warmth like the afternoon sun, only dustier. Pleasantly warm, but not strong enough to burn her skin. Perfect for a nap.

She curled on her side and watched the mushroom. Hyphae undulated in slow waving patterns. It seemed like she was watching them through a cloud of dust. She rubbed her eyes. The mushroom bumped against her side. She scratched it under its cap. Her eyes fell closed. Her breathing slowed. The mushroom purred.

Megan slept.

The Well

Somewhere, unbound by the laws of time and space, exists a wishing well. You probably haven't heard of this well, but not because it's a secret. It's just that most people who encounter it aren't around to tell the tale.

You might encounter it on the side of the road one day, or on the very top of the highest mountain. It's boundless, endless, traversing time, space and other universes effortlessly. It can exist in multiple places at once, and it can cease existing at all if it so desires.

Most people will never hear of it, even fewer will ever encounter it. You might see it flicker in the corner of your eye, only to find emptiness when you turn to look. You might stumble upon it on a holiday in a distant country, or it might one day stand in the middle of your yard. You might only ever see it in your dreams.

Don't be fooled, even in your dreams the well is very real.

If you ever encounter the well, have a good look, talk to it for a bit, give it a pat on those worn old stones. The well is lonely and there's no reason to fear it.

So long as you don't make a wish...

Don't make a wish. Boredom is the bane of the well's existence. It seeks entertainment. It knows exactly how many loopholes exist in a one-sentence contract and it will use every single one of them.

You ask it for a mansion and you find yourself a blood-thirsty creature, your mansion neighbouring a small village and its occupants brandishing torches and stakes, advancing steadily. You wonder what's the harm in wishing for a rad sword, and find yourself suddenly in a field, pulling a sword from a rock, the scrape of metal on stone ringing in your ears. You're in another world and you'll never see your family again.

The well isn't kind, it won't give you time to breathe. It takes pleasure in your panic, in your frantic efforts to figure out what's going on and what to do. That's what it lives for. From the moment your coin hits the deep waters of the well, your life is at its mercy.

Don't expect to live long beyond that point.

The River Spirit

A corpse, still fresh, drifted down the river. Soon it would become part of the current that moved it forward. Everything in the current belonged to the river, to its spirit. The spirit drifted around the corpse, examining all its features. Its murky eyes, its tangle of brown hair. She wondered what it had been like in life. Before its lungs filled with water, when it still fought for its life, clawing at the banks.

The corpse was untouched. The fish and insects hadn't dared approach yet. They would come when she laid the corpse down where she thought it would best decorate the riverbed. Somewhere soft where algae and other plants grew.

There was a sound on the banks nearby, but the spirit ignored it. The banks weren't part of her domain, weren't her concern. Only the river was, and its new occupant.

The corpse's hand tangled in strands of algae. There was blood on its fingers, stuck under its nails. She felt the creatures of the river lurking, watching them pass, roused by the smell of blood. None of them came near, but it was only a matter of time. The corpse's hand moved, its fingers seemed to be grasping for something. Comfort. Maybe it was scared. It didn't look scared. Its face was slack and peaceful, murky eyes stared sightlessly at the sky. But looks could be deceiving. She grabbed the hand, held it gently. Even softened by the water, its callouses were still apparent. It must have been a hard worker in life.

A loud crack sounded from the banks. The spirit kept her eyes on the river, pretended not to have heard the sound, but underwater she squeezed the cold hand for comfort. What happened on the banks wasn't her concern. The current sped up, driven by the spirit. Their drifting became less peaceful. Harsher turns and streams hustled the corpse, bobbing it up and down and jerking it this way and that.

The corpse jerked, pulled her hand, twisted to the side. It went against the current. The spirit looked up in confusion. A branch was caught in the corpse's shirt. She followed it with her gaze. It was thick and sturdy. Bright green leaves grew on twigs at the sides. At the other end, stood not a tree, but a human. Now she knew what the sound had been. The spirit kept a tight hold of the corpse's hand and increased the current further. She didn't want to lose it. It would be such a lovely addition to the riverbed. She already knew of the perfect place. No human would steal what was hers.

Water flowed around the corpse, moving its limbs in erratic patterns. Its shirt was pulled taut where the branch held it. While the branch bent into a strong curve, it didn't break. The human was smart to use a living branch instead of a dead one. She increased the current more. A creaking sound came from the branch. Her corpse was almost safe. The creaking became stronger. The branch bent further. And then her hand gasped only water. She watched the corpse's hand slip away from her as it broke the surface and flew out of the water.

The corpse flopped on the ground.

A ringing started up in her ears. The ever-present splash of water on rocks silenced. The spirit stared. Her corpse lay prone on the banks, eyes wide open in horror. Rivulets of water dripped from its clothes, down the rocks, back into the river. *The banks weren't part of her domain.*

The thief, a short human lady wearing a faded black robe, sat next to the corpse catching her breath. Fire burned in the spirit's eyes. A spiralling current formed around her. The lady was too preoccupied to notice. She shuffled closer and knelt next to the corpse. She clasped her hands in prayer. Her eyes closed. Long strings of muttered words drifted over the water.

The words caught in the current. Over the sound of the roiling water, the spirit caught only slivers of them. Words of flesh, life, soul and spirit. They enveloped her, drew on her magic. The foreign pull on her magic snapped her out of her furious trance. She pulled away from them, but they snatched onto her magic like hooks. She struggled against them, directed the current back into a straight line to take her away, but the words only hooked deeper. She clawed at the ground, at the algae, the weeds. Pain built the harder she tried to pull away as it tore at her magic. She was helpless to stop it. She looked at the lady in horror. What in heavens could she be doing? The lady now stood up straight, eyes still closed, arms stretched out wide. Her lips moved, the words that had the spirit caught flowed out like a song. In a flash, the lady pressed down and touched her hands to the corpse. The hooks pulled taut. Her magic tore, ripped right where hers ended and that of the river began. She was ripped from the river, onto the bank. The pain was all-consuming, she blacked out.

Water violently expelled from her lungs. She heaved staggering breaths that gurgled in her throat. Hard pats on her back helped her hack up the rest of the water. She gulped lung-fulls of cold air. Every breath burnt with excruciating pain. She struggled to open her eyes. When she finally managed it, she came face to face with the rosy face of the thief, the lady in the faded robe. The lady wiped her lanky hair away from her eyes and smiled. "How are you feeling?" she asked.

Feeling? There was an emptiness in her mind she wasn't used to. Her thoughts raced around without an anchor. She tried to focus, she grasped hold of the foreign sensations of her body. Soaking wet clothes stuck to her skin, freezing because of the cold wind. Wet hair lying flat on her head. Burning lungs. A sore throat. It was overwhelming. She shied away from it, reached out to the familiar sensations of the river.

There was a gaping void where her magic should have melded with the river. Her breaths became more panicked. The burning sensation filled her mind. Her magic bled where it was ripped apart. The river was gone, the creatures were gone. She stood on the other side of the barriers the banks had always formed.

Her rising panic was interrupted by a soft voice. "I can't believe it actually worked." The lady let out a low chuckle. Her eyes were focused intently on the spirit. Her mouth stretched into a slow grin. "My first successful revival!"

The spirit's mind wavered. She looked at her hands. Calloused skin, blood under her fingernails. Thin strands of algae tangled with her fingers. "I'm not dead," she said. The words rasped in her throat, her tongue struggled to form the words. They didn't ring true. She heard the water bash against the rocks, but she didn't feel it. A droplet of water fell from her hair.

A hand touched her knee. She looked up into the bright face of the lady. She could hardly make sense of the cheerful expression, completely incongruous with her own thoughts. "Not anymore," the lady said in a chipper voice. She radiated with pride. The spirit felt nauseous. She looked at the river. The current roiled. She wanted to calm it down, tell it everything would be alright, but nothing would penetrate the void in her mind. Her magic flailed around, searching for an anchor, but didn't find one. Tears burned in her eyes, she turned away from the sight. The lady watched her, curiosity plain on her face. "Were you dead long?"

She swallowed the lump in her throat. "I didn't die." Her voice was faint, the void in her mind all-encompassing. The lady looked at her sympathetically.

"It must be hard to wrap your mind around," the lady said. "You really did die. I used a ritual to pull your spirit back into your corpse." Her eyes shone with pride. The spirit turned away and squeezed her eyes shut. Spirits, so often conflated with souls. A falsehood spread wide among humans. A falsehood giving them the idea they could bring back the dead. The lady was a necromancer. One of those idiotic humans who thought they could play with magic. Her magic flared in anger, flailed around. It got lost in the void around the ripped edge, losing the anger in the process. She needed an anchor, her ungrounded mind was distant and hard to grasp. She squeezed her hands, tried to find some comfort in the feeling of the algae stretching around her fingers.

A hand patted on her head. "You're okay now," the lady said. The spirit opened her eyes, glared at the lady's comforting expression. She wasn't okay, and her touch didn't bring her any comfort. She slapped the hand away and stood up. Her eyes automatically moved towards the river. The water had risen higher. A duck went by, flapping its wings in a panic, trying to escape the current.

"Reverse it," the spirit said. The lady stood up in alarm. "Reverse the ritual." Surely there was a way.

"What? No!" The lady's eyes were wide. "I can't just kill you."

"You already killed me," the spirit said. The lady's face paled. She shook her head. The spirit's voice shook, "Y— you ripped me away." She gestured to the river. As she did, one of the rocks at the edge of the bank was taken by the current.

The lady stared, noticing the state of the river for the first time since fishing out the corpse. Her mouth opened and closed silently for a moment.

"That wasn't your corpse?"

The spirit's eyes flared. "My corpse? Of course it's my corpse! It was in the river, wasn't it? That means it's mine." Her chest heaved. She stood face to face with the lady, closer than she remembered. "First you stole my corpse and then you—" She couldn't get the words past her lips for a second time. "You have to reverse it."

The lady took a step back. The bottom of her robe landed in a pool of water. "I can't." Her eyes were brimming with tears. There was no hint of deception in her expression. The spirit didn't want to believe her.

"You have to!" Her voice broke with desperation. She couldn't stay like this. She was part of the river, she would go mad from the empty part of her mind, the ripped edge where her magic was supposed to meld into the river.

A wave crashed against the rocks, splashing her face with water. The lady's hair stuck to her forehead. "I don't know how," she said. Her voice was barely audible over the raging current. "I'm so sorry."

The spirit looked away from the earnest expression. It couldn't be true. The water rolled over her feet. It was cold. It was empty. She was alone. There were no snails to comfort her, no fish to make her laugh. Without them, the silence in her mind was deafening. She clasped the algae in her hands. She felt the slimy strands in her fingers, but she couldn't feel its comforting languid emotions. Her magic clawed at it to no avail. It felt dead. Her hands shook, she didn't want to feel it anymore. The strands slipped through her fingers and splashed in the water. It washed away into the river. *Everything in the current belongs to the river.*

Of course. Her eyes roved over the furious waters. Her feet moved on their own. She stumbled over a raised rock hidden under a layer of water. "No!" the lady shouted. "What if you die? What if it doesn't work?"

The current raged around her legs. She turned around from her place on the edge of the rocks. They locked eyes. "It would be better than this." She plunged into the deep.

A corpse, still fresh, drifted down the river.

Soon it would become part of the current that moved it forward.

Everything in the current belonged to the river.

Ana's Nightmares

Pig was Ana's escape from her dreams. Flimsy and deflated, the stuffing compacted by years of squishes and hugs, Pig was always there for her when she woke from those terrible nightmares. Where her dreams were filled with dread, flashes of pain, dizzying movements, Pig was pure comfort. Always the same, reliable, in her control.

Her dreams weren't always the same. Sometimes she would wake up with the memory of dry eyes pressed against rough fabric, other times it was the bruising grip of an inhumanly large hand around her torso or arm. But no matter what changed in the dreams, one thing stayed the same; She could never move. She couldn't blink, she couldn't talk, she couldn't breathe. She could only feel.

Her most hated dreams were those of darkness. In the dark, she was constricted by something she couldn't quite place. The agony of the soft yet unforgiving substance squeezing her, flattening her, contorting her body in impossible angles. But worse was the knowledge she could do nothing to help herself, nothing to end it or at least relieve the pressure. All she could do was wait. In her dreams she had no hope of waking up. In her dreams she expected it all to go on forever.

Once she dreamt of the room spinning around her, water filling her head, no air to breathe and soap stinging in her eyes. When she woke up drenched in sweat, Pig was there waiting for her on her pillow, clean and smelling fresh.

She dreamt of falling, of lying crumpled and broken at the bottom of a cliff, neck bent at an angle that made her nauseous to think about. Pig was there for her then as well. She swiped him up from the floor and sobbed into the soft worn fabric. Pig understood.

Even during the day she was haunted by the memories of being lifted into the air, forced to move her arms and legs by a hand the size of a chair, forced to speak words in a voice not her own. She had no voice of her own.

But with Pig by her side, she felt better. Pig told her it was alright. Pig hugged her when she cried. As long as she had Pig, she could forget.

This night was different. This night Ana woke up with dread pooling in her stomach, bile rising in her throat. She lay there in silence, for once not testing whether she could move, for once not opening her eyes to see if she could blink, for once not pulling Pig into her arms. She shook, her breaths sounded more like sobs. The voice… She recognised that voice. Memory after memory flashed through her mind of her playing with Pig. A violent twitch every time she heard that voice. The false deep tone she used when pretending to be Pig. Not his voice, but hers.

Shakily she switched on the light. In the light her dreams weren't real. In the light, Pig was her comfort. In the light, she looked into her Pig's eyes and saw pain.

Land's Intelligence

With an excited spring in her step, Emelia Warren followed the path towards the river. She'd wanted to explore the river for such a long time now, and finally she could. She understood why her parents didn't like her to go there of course, and some years ago she would have been terrified to get anywhere near it, but she was an adult now and could make decisions of her own. And what she decided was that her desire to explore was much bigger than any danger or fear.

Her crunching footsteps morphed into near-silent thuds as she left the gravel path in favour of grass. The path didn't get very close to the water, and close is what she wanted to get. She would be careful of course. The edges were steep and slippery, nearly impossible to escape from if you fell in.

Before long, the river came into view. She stopped at a safe distance and just watched for a moment. The river wasn't very wide, but it had a rather strong current. The water slipping over stones and dirt, shimmering in the sunlight, was mesmerising. The grass near the edge looked extra vibrant, the plants taller, the trees stronger. The river was the source of life for all the plants in the area, including her home town. As she looked at it though, even though it was the source of life, the river itself wasn't alive at all.

For as long as she could remember, the lands Emelia lived in had felt... intelligent. Here near the river, it was more palpable than ever. It wasn't any one thing, more of a combination of little things stacked together. The way the tree branches swayed in the absence of wind; The perfect distribution of plants, none competing with the other; The insects that she'd felt watching her from the moment she left the path.

She was a bit disappointed to find the river itself to be so lifeless. It was just water. There was no mystery to it, no intelligence. She always assumed... what with Elric...

His body had only been found in the river after days of searching. She'd assumed then that the river was the new interesting thing Elric had found. A new intelligence, or maybe part of the other. But now it seemed like that wasn't the case.

Maybe his brother knew what he'd meant? Emelia had never asked. It always felt insensitive to bring it up in front of Mark so shortly after his brother's death. She didn't much like thinking of her dead friend herself either. Then the family moved away and they lost contact, so Emelia would probably never know.

Well, unless she found Elric's discovery herself. That's why she wanted to explore the river after all.

She walked along the edge, careful to stay at a safe distance at all times. Although her fear had waned over the years, the memory of Elric's death was still clear. She wondered if he followed this same path along the river all those years ago. Occasionally she went a little closer to the edge to examine things that caught her eye. One time it was a bush she'd never seen before. Then there was a small bright blue bird on the other side of the water.

Then, her eye caught on some strange looking branches hidden partly behind a hill. It took her away from the river, but not very far. As she walked around it, she saw the branches were part of a particularly gnarly tree. The trunk was thick but uneven. It was twisted, curled and folded. The bark was even worse. It had completely worn off in places and where it was still there, it was chunky, uneven and misshapen. The trunk wasn't much taller than Emelia, the twisting branches adding just enough for the tree to be about double her size. The exposed roots digging into the bottom of the hill were as misshapen as the rest of it.

Emelia stepped on one and was mildly surprised it felt sturdy. The tree looked dead enough for the roots to be rotten, but that evidently wasn't the case. She stepped from root to root to get around the tree, but her path was cut off abruptly.

There was a hole. A dark opening nestled between the roots, slanting towards the hill.

Emelia backed away, inexplicably unnerved. The hole was big enough for her to crawl through if she wanted. The thought gave her pause. If she could crawl through it as an adult, what would it be like for a child? Excitement coursed through her. This was it. This must have been what Elric found. She was sure of it.

Emelia peered into the darkness, but couldn't see where it ended. She bit her lip. She wanted to know what was inside, but she knew all too well how dangerous it could be. She stepped closer again and felt along the top of the hole. The dirt was packed tightly, only a tiny stream of dust came loose. It didn't feel like it would collapse…

She took a deep breath. She could go back home to change into different clothes and grab a powerful torch, but she knew she'd lose her nerve if she did that. It was now or never.

Kneeling before the hole, she grabbed her phone and hesitated for another long moment. She should at least message her parents to let them know what she was going to do, but they would tell her to stop. Honestly, she *should* stop.

She thought about Elric, about his little body falling in the river she could hear gurgling behind her. She swallowed hard. She needed to know what he died for.

She grabbed her phone tight, turned on the torch, and crawled inside.

The ground was cold and damp under her hands and bare knees. The top of her head and back scraped along the top of the hole. Moisture dampened her t-shirt, making it cling to the skin of her back. Even fully inside, she still couldn't see where it ended. The stream of light from her phone torch lit up where the tunnel got tighter, before opening up again. She crawled forward on her hands and knees. Her neck ached from holding her head down. If it got any tighter, she would turn around. She wasn't claustrophobic by any means, but having to drag herself forward on her elbows was too much.

Then she got through the tightest point, and the tunnel opened up. To her surprise, the tunnel was big enough to stand up in. She felt along the walls and ceiling. On both, the dirt was so tightly packed together it resembled the walls of an actual house. Was this man-made? It made her feel melancholy. This really would have been an amazing hideout to play in as children. She could easily imagine her, Elric, and Mark running around here, pretending to have all sorts of adventures.

Sturdy or not, the tunnel was strangely bumpy in places. It got worse the further she went. She had to aim her phone down so she wouldn't trip. The light of her phone was weaker than she expected and had trouble penetrating the darkness, necessitating her to aim it close in front of her.

She kept expecting something to jump out at her from the void ahead, but she didn't turn around. Somehow sure her fear was unfounded. It was the silence. It was utterly silent in the tunnel. If there was something ahead, she would know, dark or not. It was reassuring in a way silence had never felt before. For someone who filled her days with music, even when trying to sleep, this comfort was new.

After a while, she noticed a pattern on the floor. White criss-crossing lines that got denser the further she went. She stopped for a moment to get a better look. It was mycelium, fungal roots she recognised from finding them under rotting logs in the forest.

She followed the white fleshy lines with her phone light and found them not only on the floor, but on the walls and ceiling as well. They converged at the bulbous outcroppings she'd thought were dirt, but now realised were mushrooms. Hard, almost wood-like mushrooms.

She moved on. The ground became increasingly squishy and the lines of mycelium became thicker and denser. She wondered how deep it went. How long would she have to dig before she would reach normal dirt? Judging by how deep her feet sunk, a long time.

A cold drop of water fell on her nose. Above her, strands of mycelium—hyphae—hung from the ceiling. Drops of water slowly gathered at their ends, before falling under their own weight. Could she be under the river?

Despite the moist atmosphere, the air was growing—well, not exactly stale. It still smelt fresh, but there was a dustiness to it.

Grainy might be a better word.

It got worse. Until her nose was stuffed with the damp air. Fleetingly she considered if it could be toxic, but she didn't feel bad and dismissed the thought. Besides, she didn't want to turn around now that she was so close to the end.

She could feel it. Wherever the tunnel was leading her to, it was close.

When her nose became too clogged to breathe through and the damp dust lay thick on her tongue, she saw it. She froze. She didn't breathe, she didn't blink.

The tunnel opened up into a room. The walls, ceiling and floor were so packed with mycelium they were completely white. In the middle of the room stood a platform reminiscent of the marble stands of mausoleums. An apt comparison considering the corpse lying upon it.

Emelia couldn't seem to turn her phone away from the sight. The feet were all bone, nearly all flesh rotten away in the moist environment. Fluffy mould grew between the ligaments and joints of the toes where some leftover flesh still rotted. But that wasn't the worst of it.

All over, the rotten flesh was replaced by mycelium and small, white, almost luminescent mushrooms. Hyphal strings ran between the corpse and the walls and ceiling, most at the head.

The corpse stirred.

Emelia stared, too terrified to even think. The corpse rose slowly, lifted by the strings in the ceiling. It floated there, upright, staring at Emelia with mushroom-filled eye-sockets. Its arms lazily stretched to either side. Stringy hair waved around its head, dancing in a current that didn't exist.

Like tree branches on wind-still days...

Emelia knew. This being was the truth of the intelligence she'd always observed. Not just an intelligence, but something... that might have once been human.

She ran, aided by the squishy floor under her feet. The concept of a nebulous intelligence controlling the land around her was interesting, beautiful, almost comforting. Seeing the inhuman, unnatural thing at its centre was something else.

Wet hanging strands slapped in her face as she sped through the tunnel. She didn't watch where she stepped. She crushed the bulbous fungi under her feet, nearly tripped on one too sturdy to break. She didn't care. She needed to get out, nothing else mattered.

A light appeared ahead of her. In her desperation, she hadn't even noticed she dropped her phone. She fell to her knees and crawled through the last tight bit of the tunnel.

The outside light was blinding, but she kept running. She went in the direction of town, but she was disoriented. She just managed to stop herself when her eyes adjusted to the light and she saw she was headed straight for the river.

The water glistened in the light of the setting sun. She slumped on the riverbed, suddenly too exhausted to continue her sprint. Her legs ached, her lungs heaved. She tried to catch her breath, but it was difficult with her clogged nose. The water rushed by, unmoved by her near plunge. She thought of Elric's body, drifting by on the current.

When she finally got home, she paused in the doorway for a long moment, watching her father puttering around in the kitchen. She wanted to tell him, tell him and her mother about the monster under the river, the thing that killed Elric. But she couldn't. They would never believe her.

She took a deep breath and entered, giving her father a strained smile as she passed him. "Hey love, had a good walk?" he asked.

"Yeah... just going to take a shower now." Her voice was strained, but hopefully he'd just chalk it up to her stuffed nose.

The hot water was heaven on her cold skin. She washed off a layer of dust and grime she hadn't even noticed was there. Once she stepped out, she quickly dried her hands and face so she could grab a piece of paper to blow her nose into.

The relief of being able to breathe again didn't last long, as when she looked at the paper there was no snot or even dust, but white fleshy hyphal strands.

Fenced in

I've always thought trees had a certain energy to them. Nothing outright magical, or at least, nothing we as humans could harness as magic.

When you stand next to one of those old, huge trees—a trunk at least twice as wide as you are, thick branches reaching for the sky, curling and twisting high above—you stand there close to the stem and look up, and that's when you feel it; this energy, this enormity.

It's so difficult to describe, but I'm sure I'm not the only one. I've seen others stare up when underneath a tree, and you can just see it in their expression.

It's certainly not as prevalent with the smaller trees. I think it develops as the tree matures. If you can catch the energy of a younger tree, you'll feel the difference. It feels less solid, malleable.

But it's difficult to feel this energy. You can almost see it in the way their branches sway in the wind, but you can never *feel* it because you can't get close enough. There's always those damn fences in the way.

I know what they say, what they want me to believe. That they're there to support the tree while its root system develops enough to hold it upright. It might even be true to a certain extent. But that doesn't explain the trees that have been fenced in for years.

You can say it's just laziness. Local governments not bothering to remove the fences when they're not needed anymore, but I don't believe that. I think it's done on purpose. It can't be a coincidence that the energy of wild unchained trees feels so different from the ones trapped by humans.

But why? Why would they trap a tree in a wooden fence? Why would they want to affect their energy? I don't know. I don't know why trees need to be trapped, but it's not just the tiny ones. It's bigger ones as well.

They're few and far between, but sometimes you'll find one standing in the middle of a field. Huge, majestic, intimidating, with an aura so intense you can almost feel it from the road. They're beautiful. Their branches are fanned out in such a perfect dome you just know they've been standing alone in that field for their whole life.

But their magnificent beauty is tainted by the hardwood fence surrounding them. Their energy stifled. I sometimes wonder if it's some sort of cruel joke to trap them in the dead remains of their kind. It's like trapping a human in a cage made of bone and desiccated flesh.

I try to keep my distance from those trees. Not because I don't like them, but just… I saw something once, in the forest near where I live. You can imagine I often walk through the forest with my love for trees and nature. I know my usual route so well I could walk it blindfolded. I used to go out at night as well.

I don't anymore.

The forest has many clearings in which farmers either grow corn or raise animals. I like the ones with animals better, they often have a more naturalistic look.

I walked past one of those and saw the usual trees standing there. Three of them, still relatively small, all with a fence around them despite the fact they've all stood there for half a decade by now. I pity them, trapped the way they are in their fences while their brethren around them in the forest are free to stand unrestricted.

Nothing looked abnormal then, but on my way back home when I walked past the same field, one of the fences stood empty.

I paused and looked around the field. I thought I'd just missed the empty fence earlier and there would still be three other trees, but no. There were only two.

I'm not embarrassed to say I freaked out. I resumed my walk at a much faster pace than before, intent on getting out of the forest as soon as possible. All the while my mind tried to come up with all sorts of rational explanations.

None of them held up. They were all more convoluted than the truth, and I'm not one to believe a complicated explanation over a simpler one. I felt eyes following me. More than just eyes, *something* was following me.

I increased my pace. I thought I heard footsteps behind me, but when I looked there was nothing. The bushes beside me rustled.

Just a bird, a tree would never fit—could it? The bush was placed on a slope, it wasn't impossible...

I kept walking faster. I never resorted to outright running, somehow convinced that was a step too far in going along with my delusions. I should have run. It wasn't a delusion.

I was lucky. I wasn't caught by whatever followed me, although there were moments I was sure it was a close call. I didn't slow down even when I left the forest, only allowing myself to pause and catch my breath once I'd pulled my front door closed behind me.

It took me a while before I dared enter the forest again. It's been six months, but I still don't go there at night.

I do still go past the same field. I should be watching the two remaining trees closely, waiting for any unnatural movement... but my eyes keep lingering on the still empty fence.

I don't know why we trap trees with fences. I don't believe the trees mean us harm... but I do know I don't want to be in the path of a tree that escaped its human-made prison.

Innocent if you drown

I work for a diving company. Not one of those that teaches people how to dive, but one that works for hire to clean up lakes and moats and things like that.

We were diving in an old lake a few kilometres away from the nearest city. I won't tell you the name, since I don't want to tarnish its reputation once it opens to the public.

It used to be on private property, but it was recently bought by the city to turn into a recreational area. That's why we were hired to clean the lake of any dangerous debris.

The water itself wasn't anything remarkable. It was already murky before we even stepped in it and there was a thin layer of soft organic material on the bottom which was easily stirred up by our flippers.

The rest of the crew grumbled about bad vision as we put on our equipment. Hector (not his real name) complained loudest of all. He'd cut his head badly last time we dove under these conditions.

I, on the other hand, was excited to see what this lake had in store for us. Although the lake looked fairly normal, the area around it spoke of how old the place was.

The trees around the lake were all at least two metres wide, many even wider. The small private forest the lake was located in had been left to itself for years and the forest floor was covered in shrubs and fallen trees.

So yeah, I was in a great mood. The terrible vision wouldn't deter me. Old places like this always held some interesting secrets.

We started to comb the bottom near where we'd set up on the beach and gradually moved further back. Sure enough, the vision was so bad I could hardly see more than a meter in front of me. To my disappointment, we didn't find anything interesting for the first hour.

Only once we hit deeper water further away from the beach, did we start to find stuff. Mike found a broach, Hector found the shell of a saltwater snail of all things, and Violet discovered a whole area filled with rare plants.

Of course *I* didn't find anything at all in the hours before we left the water for lunch. While eating, we examined the broach and shell. Like Hector said, it was definitely from a salt water creature. We had a bit of fun speculating how it got here. 'Theories' ranged from the lake once having been connected to the ocean, to someone just having thrown it in. I tuned out of the conversation once Violet and Hector began to debate about tectonic movements and shells found on mountains or something.

Instead, I asked Mike if I could see that broach. It was quite big. About 8 cm in diameter, nearly covering my whole palm. The edges were a delicate frilly gold, dulled from the muck on the bottom of the lake. In the middle sat a big, oval stone that shone like a rainbow in the sunlight.

Mike said it was probably Victorian. I'm not an antique jewellery expert, so I took his word on it. Regardless of its age, it was beautiful and a good find whether it was worth something or not.

After lunch, we switched up our formation. I continued where Mike left off, Mike where Hector left off, etc. We found some more trinkets over the next few hours, but nothing big.

I complained about being the only one who hadn't found anything. I guess I shouldn't have, considering...

Well, about two hours in I saw what I thought was some darkened dead stringy algae. Until I saw the human head it was attached to.

Finding bodies was never pleasant, no matter how many times it happened. It didn't help that they were often bloated and halfway rotten and or eaten by fish. At times they were nearly unrecognisable as human. But not this one.

It was the body of a woman, floating upright and looking like she just jumped in. Only her clothes looked more normal for a body that's been underwater for a while, tattered and delicate.

Once I had my heart rate under control, I notified the others. Mike went out to call the police and Violet promised to keep me company while we waited. We all knew the protocol by now. The most important rule: Never leave the body alone. You never knew where they could drift off and then it could take days or even weeks to find it again.

This is my least favourite part of the job. Staying with a corpse, in the murky waters of some lake, alone. I tried to focus on the water beyond, where Violet would soon be coming from, but the corpse kept grabbing my attention.

It was strange enough that it looked so fresh, but it behaved weirdly as well. It didn't move, only bobbed in place in the gentle currents created by my flippers. It was like she was stuck in place.

I looked closer, and my movement caused her skirt to move away from her ankle. She was handcuffed to a large rock.

I had to fight the bile rising in my throat. The mere idea of being stuck underwater, free to move but unable to escape, desperately trying to claw up to breathable air... The skin around her ankle was bruised and I'm pretty sure it was twisted, if not broken.

For the first time in years, my breath came short. My mask felt constricting, the tube leading from it too thin. Luckily that's when Violet showed up. I don't think I've ever been so grateful for some simple human company. She managed to calm me down, and then examined the body herself.

"That's quite an odd handcuff, isn't it?" she said.

I had my back to the corpse to prevent myself from panicking again, but her question had me turn around and look at the handcuff again. Violet was right. What I'd failed to notice in my panic, was that the handcuffs were of a very old design.

I'd found handcuffs before on earlier dives, and taken an interest in their history. From what I could tell through the rust, these were from around the 19th century, or more likely, a replica of the 19th-century ones.

Well, that's what I thought at the time at least.

Looking at them really made me want to take them off. It felt wrong somehow to just leave her be like that, chained to the bottom of the lake. But according to protocol we couldn't disturb what was a possible crime scene.

The two of us stayed with the corpse for more than half an hour while we waited for the police to arrive. We distracted ourselves by talking. Hector joined in as well from where he was still searching the lake.

I was glad for the police to arrive with their own diving team. After they took their pictures, I was very happy to help them hack away the chains tied around the rock. The metal gave way easily to a bit of blunt force. Violet and I helped drag the body out whenever necessary, but left most of it to the people trained for this kind of thing.

When we waded onto the beach and laid her down in the sand, I thought that was the end of it. The police would take her to the coroner and we might or might not hear about it on the news in a few days.

Then the woman coughed.

She convulsed on the ground, her lungs heaving to expel all the water. The police officers moved to help her, but I just stood there, staring. I was sure she was dead, I'd been with her underwater for nearly an hour! There was no way. And yet she was alive.

As her sputtering calmed down, she pulled her knees up to her chest. The movement disturbed the chains still attached to her ankle, causing them to rattle. I could almost feel the full-body shudder that went through her before she started to scream.

I jumped into action, nearly forgetting to pull off my flippers before sprinting to the toolbox where I grabbed a pair of pliers. When I got back, the woman had stopped screaming but was still shaking violently. I was far more out of breath than I should have been from the short distance, and I'm sure I saw the police officers breathe too quickly as well.

She looked at me when I knelt next to her. Her eyes were bright green and clearer than I expected. I didn't smile at her, or tried to comfort her as I normally would in similar circumstances. I was too freaked out to bother with any of that. I only knew that if I had gone through what she had, I would want those chains off as soon as possible. The cuff broke as easily as the chains. It was rusted through almost completely.

She hissed as I jostled her ankle when I pulled the thing off. It was obviously broken. But she didn't scream again and her shaking stopped. My breathing came easier as well. When I looked up, she was still watching me, this time calmer, but no less wary. Her eyes were still green, but I had a hard time finding that startling quality they had before.

She was rushed to the hospital soon after. We were left without any information, only able to speculate on how any of this just happened.

Violet, ever the optimist, chalked it up to some kind of

medical miracle. Hector told her not to be ridiculous, but didn't offer an explanation himself. Mike was the one who gave voice to my own thoughts, "Reminds me of the witch-hunts."

I thought of those bright, almost glowing eyes that suddenly dulled to a regular green. I took a deep breath to counter the phantom feeling of tightness in my lungs.

We didn't hear anything else about the situation. I went to the hospital the next day to see if I could talk to her, but the hospital staff didn't have a clue who I was talking about. There was nothing about it in the news later either. I'd wonder if it was just a bad dream if the others didn't remember it as well.

Whatever the case, I hope she's doing well, wherever she is.

Dear Apothecary

Dear Apothecary,

A month ago my husband Eustace purchased a bag of mushroom seeds from your store. He was delighted at first, and the mushrooms grew fast and looked surprisingly nice, the latter of which I was most happy about.

Now, Eustace would write you himself, but he is currently weeping in his office. The mushrooms will not glow, he informs me.

I will be frank, I do not know what to make of this. I suspect he merely misread your 'growing' instructions as 'glowing' instructions, but he assures me you said yourself that the mushrooms would glow.

I am sorry to say I do not know what I am asking you for. New instructions? New mushrooms? An apology? Just, anything that will end this ridiculous whining. He is acting like a child!

Please respond with the utmost urgency.

Best regards,

Nichol Packard

Dear Mrs Packard,

I remember Mr Packard. I did tell him the mushrooms

only glow for people they like. It seems the mushrooms dislike Mr Packard's whining as much as you do.

In nature, these mushrooms glow just because they like to glow, but they are very proud creatures and will not tolerate anyone they dislike seeing their glow.

You could try telling him this, but I assume by his great upset that he has already figured out the mushrooms simply dislike him. As I told him before he purchased them, you can bring them back to the store, I will even give you back half of what Mr Packard originally paid for them. You could also plant them outside in nature where they will not be bothered by people they do not like. Maybe if you plant them outside they will start liking you enough to keep glowing when you and your husband are around.

Take action with the utmost urgency, the mushrooms do not like it when they cannot glow.

Best regards,

Apothecary

PS They're called mushroom spores, not seeds.

Dear Apothecary,

I thank you for your reply, although I am sad to say even your urgent response came too late for my husband.

The good news is that the mushrooms glow now when I watch them in the garden. I found them a moist shady spot where that most lovely shade of orange can be seen even on the sunniest of days. I find a lot of joy in watching them.

I planted them in Eustace's least favourite spot in the garden, you know. Where he now rests permanently. It is what the mushrooms wanted.

I will surely come back to your shop in the future.

Best regards,

Nichol Packard

Glow beneath the leaves

It was a sunny day. Summer sat on her veranda enjoying the sun in the morning. It was the beginning of spring and one of the first of such sunny days in a long time.

It was a year since Dan's death in a house fire, and for the first time she thought she might be feeling a little more herself again.

The sun on her skin felt heavenly. The warmth seeped into her. Through her skin and clothes until she was as warm as in front of her fireplace. Moving into this old country house a month ago had done her good.

Then a shadow passed over the garden. Summer frowned and pulled her cardigan over her shoulders. She looked up to see a dark grey cloud covering the sun. It wasn't big, but it moved agonisingly slow.

She slumped back in her chair with a sigh. She stared over her shadow-cast garden.

The flowers were budding, some were even in bloom already. She saw a bumblebee buzzing around over a purple flower.

Then she noticed something odd, a glow coming from underneath a plant. A warm orange. She didn't think she had any lamps placed underneath her flowers. Maybe it was from the previous owners? She decided to check it out.

The damp grass tickled her bare feet as she walked. She knelt in front of the plant and gently pushed the leaves out of the way.

She gasped. It was a mushroom. A glowing mushroom. She stared at it, hardly believing what she was seeing. A long delicate stem, topped with a gently curving cap. The glow came from underneath the cap, but was strong enough to shine through the membrane and show off the spore chambers and a few air bubbles.

Summer stared, and stared, until she realised she was crying and wiped at her eyes. She'd never seen something this beautiful, this wonderful, this amazing. And it was in her garden. *Her* garden. All for her. She sniffled and carefully reached out a hand to touch the cap. It felt like any mushroom, soft and silky.

She sat there for a long time, just watching it, enjoying how the glow strengthened when the sun shone on it, as if competing with the sun itself. Eventually, the sky darkened, and Summer was left watching the only speck of light in the darkness of her garden. High in the sky, the stars shone bright and numerous, so many more than she ever saw when she lived in the city. But she wasn't watching them tonight. That one little mushroom held all her attention.

"Thank you," she whispered at it as she went inside for the night.

Warehouse Worker

It was like stepping into another world. A world made of concrete and metal. The shelves stood like towers, or maybe hulking trees growing out of the cement floor. The sorting machine moved around, within, between, them like scuttling insects high in the canopy.

The whole thing—individual shelves coming together as one hulking mass—creaked and swayed. It was like standing on a ship, only, from your earlier entrance, you were sure the warehouse stood on firm ground.

Behind you, the workers shuffled, rubber soles shifting on rough concrete. You pressed your lips together. "What am I supposed to be helping with?" you asked, glancing behind you.

"Manpower," a burly worker said, joining you at the front. "We need more people."

You eyed the big shelves of metal, parts moving automatically, pushing crates around, carrying them where they needed to be. "In a place where everything runs by itself?"

"Yes."

Something rumbled in the distance. Wheels, maybe, or gears. A loud whistle from the same direction. The workers jumped, and three sprinted there with nervous, even fearful expressions. Their steps echoed on the cement floor long after they vanished from view.

"So, what exactly am I meant to do?"

The burly worker shook his head. "Nothing, not yet." His voice took on a peculiar tone you couldn't decipher. He continued, though it was so low you weren't sure you were meant to hear, "Sending in more people."

"Sending them to do what?" It wasn't like they were low on workers. Even with three vanished to places unknown and various others puttering around in the area, there still was a whole group at your back, doing nothing.

The worker didn't answer. You scoffed and turned away. Bastard. Suppose you were just meant to stand around then? Nothing to do, and no conversation either apparently.

Another rumble, followed by a yell. "What was that?" you asked.

"Don't worry about it," the burly worker said blandly.

You looked at the other workers, who looked equally unconcerned. "Someone screamed."

"It was just the machine. Nothing to worry about."

As if in answer, the shelves near you scraped and groaned. The sound swept through the warehouse like a wave, ending where the scream came from. You looked to the worker, who stared blankly ahead. He didn't seem to be looking at anything, let alone planning to actually do something. Frustrated, you turned and stalked off to where the nearest workers were muttering over a crate. Anything better than just standing there like a statue. But as you came closer, the discussion looked less and less work-related.

"Something wrong?" you asked.

"Everything's wrong," said a spectacled worker with a shaking voice. "It's going all wrong!"

The other worker, this one with a fierce beard, hissed and hit his companion on the arm. "Shut it. Don't let it hear you."

You watched the interaction in bafflement. "It?"

The bearded worker glared and mimed a zipper being closed over his mouth, but the spectacled one didn't heed his warning. He leaned into your space until you could see not just his hands, but even his eyes shaking in fear. "The warehouse," he whispered, "The machine."

The bearded worker growled, but any menace it might have had was betrayed by his rapidly paling face. He stormed off, clipping your shoulder as he went past. You were sure you heard a muttered 'lost cause' before his steps faded in the distance.

You laughed uneasily. "A warehouse can't hear," you said, voice strained.

The worker's eyes shifted from side to side behind his spectacles. "It can. This one can. It hears, it watches, it moves." He suddenly gripped your arms, fingers turning white from the force. It hurt. His eyes were manic. "It *lives*."

You shook your head and stepped back out of the worker's hold. The man was mad. Why was he still here? He was obviously unfit for work. But then again, all of the workers here seemed off. Near the entrance still stood the procession that'd 'welcomed' you. Just standing, staring, not even talking among themselves. Stationed throughout the place were others, instead of blank, these ones were fearful, so tense their movements seemed robotic. It gave you the creeps. You wanted your phone, to call someone, or just as a distraction, it didn't matter. But you'd had to leave it behind in a locker. Like you weren't trusted to do your job (whatever that might be) without the possible distraction of the internet. ~~Or they didn't want you to call for help.~~

The machine rolled past, close to the spectacled worker's back. Were the shelves this close before? They hadn't moved. The worker shrieked and ran away in a blind panic, deeper into the forest of shelves.

You stumbled back away from the shelves on shaky legs.

Your balance was all off, like the world around you had tilted to the left. The shelves rattled as the machine hurtled past, carrying enough weight in metal to squash you like a bug.

The fear, the workers, the machine, It didn't make any sense. This wasn't supposed to—

The world tilted again, this time to the right.

Not here, not in the middle of the fucking country. You weren't anywhere close to the sea.

There this was normal, *there* this was fine. Machines coming alive on the swaying of the waves. Ships developing a mind of their own as they listened to the whispers of the deep. The engine rumbling, screeching, demanding fuel, demanding power, demanding *life.*

But not here. Not here far away from it all, in a massive warehouse in the middle of the country. The only connection to the sea was—

It was—

Oh no.

The shelves towered, hulking metal structures in a world of concrete. The shelves carried crates full of metal themselves. Sheets as thick as castle walls, screws the length of thigh bones, pipes and tubes an army could march through.

All tiny bits meant for bigger things. Parts of massive machines. *Parts of engines. Ship engines.*

The workers watched dispassionately as you stumbled toward them, falling and having to use those infernal shelves to lean on every time the world around you swayed. The waves of the deep so entranced in the metal it bled through to the warehouse itself, giving it life.

The machine screamed around you, rumbled under your clutching hand, louder and louder. For a moment, the dispassion of the workers shifted, a spark of something appeared in their eyes. One winced in anticipation, eyes trained behind y—

.

.

.

It was just the machine. Nothing to worry about.

A Swarm

A Fly

The door opened before Shane could reach for the bell. A woman with wavy chestnut coloured hair stood in the door opening, a bright smile on her face. "I saw you walk over," Danielle said. Shane smiled back, always happy to see his friend.

Danielle let him in, and Shane breathed in the cooler air in relief. The summer was exceptionally warm this year, and today especially.

A cloud of water sprayed out of a humidifier standing on top of the wooden plant shelf in the hallway. Shane stopped for a moment and relished in the cool droplets falling on his face. Danielle looked back at him and laughed. "Stop that, I'll give you something cool to drink."

He rushed after her, through the plant-filled living room and into the kitchen. Danielle's entire house was like an oasis, plants included. Any space that wasn't filled with furniture was covered in plants. Long vines with round bright green leaves hung down from the top kitchen cupboards. The counter was filled with herbs and flowers in all kinds of colours.

Despite the sunlight streaming in through the big windows, the house wasn't nearly as hot as Shane's was at the moment. Danielle didn't have any air conditioning, but the frequent watering of her plants and the humidifiers spread throughout her house made for a delightfully refreshing temperature.

She dodged his attempt to grab one of the glasses out of her hand and moved into the living room. He followed.

She set the glasses on the stone table and flopped back onto the worn leather sofa. Shane sat down in his favourite spot, the armchair directly across from her, and pulled his glass towards him. Iced tea. He closed his eyes. Amazing.

When he opened his eyes and put the empty glass back on the table, he saw Danielle was holding something. He looked at her questioningly.

She held the item up. It was a plant. He should have known. Danielle nearly always had a new plant to show him. "What is it?" It was quite different from her normal plants. The leaves were dark green and sharp. There were thorns on the stems.

"A black rose!" she said excitedly. "Isn't it gorgeous?" It was then that Shane noticed the flowers, half-hidden between the dark leaves. The petals were not actually black of course, but without the sunlight, he wouldn't have been able to see the purple sheen.

The flowers were small, proportional to the tiny plant. The pot it was in was about the size of a teacup, and was a sleek dark purple. Danielle looked at him expectingly. "It's beautiful," he said honestly.

She grinned widely. "I got it from the hardware store." She had been raving about the new hardware store just out of town for the entirety of the last week, it apparently had rare plants she couldn't find anywhere else.

She set the plant in the middle of the big table. It should have looked ridiculous, such a tiny thing on that big slab of rock, but it didn't. There was an elegance to it that you wouldn't usually find in Danielle's house. Not that her house wasn't elegant of course, he would never even think that. But hers was a different sort of elegance. The effortless kind that was best exemplified in his friend's hair, which she never styled but which always looked perfect anyway.

As Danielle continued to talk, Shane squinted at the little plant. There, he hadn't been imagining it. Something moved on the soil.

"Oh no, there's a fly in it," he said. Danielle waved him off.

"I noticed. A bit irritating, but the spiders will take care of it."

Shane nodded. He looked at one of the corners of the living room where a fat spider languished in its web. Danielle was probably the only person in the world who could make spiders and webs in her house look good instead of unkempt.

"So, you really like the rose?"

Shane nodded, a bit unsure. "Yeah, like I said, I like it. Why?"

"No reason," she said quickly, "I was just curious."

"Well, I love the colours. It's very elegant, especially in that pot." He smiled. "It looks perfect there on the table, you should keep it there."

Danielle smiled a little secretively. "Sure, I'll keep that in mind."

They spent the rest of the afternoon there languishing in the sun. By the end, Shane knew exactly which plants she was planning to buy when her next paycheck came in.

A Couple of Flies

Shane fluttered his hand in front of his face, waving a tiny fly out of his vision. "Spiders weren't hungry?" He once again sat in his favourite armchair, Danielle across from him on the sofa, sunlight from the window casting strange shadows on her face through the leaves of her monstera plant.

She shook her head. "Oh no, they were hungry alright. I saw one stuck in a web, but there must have been more I didn't see at first."

The ice cubes in his coffee clinked together as he took a sip. "Maybe you should get some pesticide, get rid of them before they become a real problem."

"Maybe." Offhandedly she pressed her finger on the table, squishing a fly on the stone surface. "I don't want to use poison inside the house. They're annoying, but they don't hurt me." Next to her hand lay a dried flower that must have fallen off the small rose bush. Shane was happy she kept the plant on the table, it really looked good there. "Besides, it's good food for the spiders, so I don't mind too much."

In the corner of the room an even fatter spider than last week sat in a web speckled with little dots; the desiccated remains of all the flies it sucked dry. Despite the number of flies dead in that web, there were still a few hovering around in the room. Shane's gaze tracked one crawling in the soil of Danielle's beloved palm tree. "You should consider it."

"D'you think I can still save it?" Danielle asked. Shane looked at the pitiful rose bush. The flowers had withered weeks ago, only a single bud still hung limp between the wilting leaves.

"Doubtful."

Danielle slumped on the sofa. Even the proud palm and enormous monstera flanking her throne had lost their lush shine. Or maybe that was just the lack of sun. "I bought it for you, you know?"

"You did?"

"I thought it would look just perfect in your house. You could really use a plant in there. But now… I feel so useless. If I can't even keep it alive, what was the point of bringing all those stupid flies into my home?"

Danielle wasn't the only one who felt useless. This happened all because she wanted to give him a gift? He was so touched, and he didn't even know how to comfort her. Awkwardly, he offered, "For the spiders?"

Danielle hummed noncommittally. "Come to think of it, I haven't seen my spiders in a while."

Huh, Shane hadn't noticed it yet either, but now that he looked, he saw the corners of the room were all empty. Not even an abandoned web was left to offer proof of the fat spider that had lived there for months.

"They'll come out again come autumn," he said. The clean corners made him uneasy. They were... immaculate. Lifeless. They reminded him of his own home.

"True." Her eyes lit up. She shot up and pressed her finger on the table with a vindictive grin. That was the third squished fly in the past fifteen minutes.

"Talking about autumn," she said as she relaxed back into the sofa, "I need to start going to the forest more, gather some acorns and pinecones. I need something new in the hallway. And I guess the table here needs something decorative as well. Maybe a pumpkin..."

He listened contently to Danielle's ramble about autumn decorations, occasionally interspersed with another squished fly.

Shane brushed the dirty strands of spiderweb off the wood with his shoe. It was mostly pine needles caught in it and some seed husks, but he didn't want to risk grasping right where a spider sat.

He inspected the other sides of the quarter log, then placed it on his pile. That would be enough for now. Huffing with exertion, he lifted the pile in his arms and carried it to the back door.

He pressed the handle down with his elbow and pushed inside. His shoes smeared dirt across his dark hardwood floor. He walked past the granite kitchen counters, into his living room.

The wood clattered on the floor. He knelt next to the pile and neatly stacked them under the fireplace. There, that should be enough for a couple of weeks.

Autumn had come early and the air in his house was chilly. Despite his general preference for summer, he was happy about the change of season. Not even the bright summer sun could compare to the comforting warmth of his fireplace.

An hour later the living room had warmed up considerably. He stared into the flames, content to let his mind wander.

This spot here, on the armchair in front of the fireplace, was his favourite spot in the house. While he loved the work the designer did, he sometimes felt it was lacking something. But this corner of the living room was perfect. The fireplace radiated the warmth the other rooms lacked. The textured stone added just the right visual interest. The window next to it preventing it from becoming too dark and secluded while not being so big as to stop it from being cosy.

The wood popped, and a spider crawled out in a panic. He wasn't surprised, no matter how thoroughly he inspected the wood, there would always be a few he missed.

He thought of Danielle, of her empty corners. Maybe she would appreciate a new spider?

A Bunch of Flies

Shane took his finger off the doorbell after two seconds. He put the jar between his hands again and waited patiently for Danielle to open the door.

When the door opened, he held the spider jar in front of him.

"Shane! I wasn't expecting you to— What's this?"

He grinned. "I got you a spider!"

He lowered the jar so he could see her face. She had her hair pulled up into a messy knot on top of her head. Her eyes were bright. A high pitched noise escaped her. "Oh! this is great! We'll put it in my office..." She grabbed Shane's arm and dragged him inside. "The flies have been driving me up the wall!"

She let go of his arm halfway through the hallway. Without the sun shining through the door windows, the hallway was dark. She continued to the stairs and he followed, amused by her enthusiasm.

They passed the paintings of sunny landscapes in the upstairs hallway. If only he could have both the warm brightness of the sun and the cosiness of his fireplace at once.

He snapped out of it when something hit his forehead. Before he could feel for it, he saw the fly already floating away. He smiled down at the spider in the jar. Revenge would be sweet. Well, sweet for the spider at least.

Danielle held up her hands for the jar when they reached the office. Shane gave it to her and rubbed his hands together, only now realising how cold the glass had gotten. He was starting to regret not putting on a coat. It usually wasn't necessary for the short walk from his house to hers, but it was really cold here.

"Sorry, the radiator's been having some trouble," She explained, "I'm considering getting an electric one for in here, but they tend to kill any humidity."

Shane rolled his eyes. "Better a little less humidity than you freezing to death in your office."

"Ha ha," she said. "Give me a hand, will you?" Shane helped her climb onto her desk. Around her feet, he noticed multiple squished flies on the wood.

"I can see why they're driving you up the wall, how many are there here? Five?"

"Seven." She strained to open the jar lid. Shane held out

his hand. "All from yesterday." She handed the jar to him. The lid was on tight, but he did a good job of making it look effortless.

"Seven in one day?" He handed the jar back. She put it on the plank closest to the ceiling corner, then jumped from the desk, her hand on his for balance.

She smiled at him, and Shane was helpless not to answer it with a grin of his own. "Thanks."

"You're welcome."

They moved back through the hallway in the direction of the stairs. As they walked in contented silence, Shane noticed a strange static coming from behind the walls, like Danielle had forgotten to turn off her television. He put his hands in his pockets to stave off the cold. "Isn't the cold bad for your plants as well?"

She hummed. "Not ideal for the tropical ones, but it's better than low humidity."

Halfway down the stairs, a resounding clap blasted through the house. With his heart in his throat, it took Shane a few moments to realise it was just the sound of the house adjusting to the warmth of the radiator. Danielle didn't react to it.

A little breathless from the scare, he said, "I don't think it's supposed to be that loud. My house doesn't do this you know."

"What? Oh, that." She was so unconcerned Shane wondered if she'd heard the noise at all. "I never got those renovations done."

He supposed that Danielle's house did look a little saggier than the other houses in the street. The roof concaved in the middle, not much, but enough to notice when you saw it through your window every day.

"You should have it checked." He waved another fly out of his face. "And finally call an exterminator while you're at it."

She didn't have to turn around for him to see her rolling her eyes. "And kill the spider you just generously gave me? No way."

He sighed. "Should I bring you the others that come out of the fire as well then?"

"Yes please!"

A Swarm

Shane slowly lowered the spider-jar when he caught the look on Danielle's face. She was pale, her eyes were red and underlined with dark bags. "Danielle?"

Her smile was unconvincing. "Come in."

The hallway was even darker than it normally was on overcast days. The little autumn decorations on the table against the wall were starting to rot, and multiple flies crawled around on the squash pumpkin.

Danielle sat down in her usual seat first. The leaves of the monstera to her left were yellowing and the stem of the palm on her other side was wrinkly and dry.

Shane didn't waste any time once he sat down. "What's wrong?"

A harsh laugh, a sound that he'd never heard her make before. "The flies of course. What else could it be? They— " She swallowed. "The spiders are all gone." Shane looked around. The two spiders they'd left in the living room in past week were gone.

He waited, not understanding why that would upset her this much. He tapped on the lid of the jar. Spiders vanish all the time, that's just what they do.

"Yesterday, there was only one left. I expected them to move around, but to vanish completely?" She shook her head. "I stayed awake last night. I had to see if they'd just ran off after all." She laughed again. "It didn't run."

Shane sat up straighter at the dark tone of her voice.

"The web was already covered in flies when I began to watch. Some were dead, others still flailing around. There were far more than the spider could ever need. It was gorging itself on a particularly fat one. You'd expect the supply of flies to run out at some point, but they just kept coming. As if the web was covered in syrup! Even the spider got uneasy. It dropped the one it was eating before he finished and moved around, killing a few of the ones still flailing.

"Still more flies came. The spider moved to the edge of its web. I thought that was it. The spiders all vanished because the flies freaked them out. But before it could leave, they began to land on the spider itself."

She paused for a moment, lost in the memory. Shane stared at her, not sure if he should believe it, not wanting to believe it, but Danielle had never lied to him before. She continued.

"The spider struggled of course, but there were so many. I couldn't see what was happening. One moment two or three were on the spider, the next they covered the whole thing." She shuddered. "I couldn't move, couldn't do anything. I just stared at the writhing mass for what must have been minutes.

"When—" She wiped at her eyes. "When they flew away the spider was gone."

Silence fell between them. He knew she wasn't lying, but did that mean she was telling the truth? He searched her face for signs of insanity. She was clearly in distress and hadn't slept either. Her eyes were red-rimmed. She sniffled, looked at him, eyes begging him to believe her.

He nodded. "What are you going to do about it?" He turned the jar in his hands, swiped a fly off the glass.

Her voice wobbled. "I called an exterminator. I don't think any pesticide I could get my hands on would work."

He hesitated. "Your plants?"

"They said they have something that shouldn't harm them, but they couldn't guarantee anything."

Anticipating the tears already forming in her eyes, Shane quickly asked her, "Do you want to stay at my place? You can stay as long as you want."

She wiped at her eyes and nodded. "That would be nice."

Shane pressed down and turned the stove button. The clicks of the built-in lighter were quickly replaced by the rushing of the fire. He turned the dial back a little and put on the kettle. After comforting Danielle for some time, he went home to prepare tea while she gathered her essentials.

The exterminator would come tomorrow, but Danielle didn't fancy staying with the flies another night. She wouldn't be able to sleep, she said.

He was happy to be home. The counters were clean, the air warm and dry. No flies in sight. Not even the fruit bowl had any fruit flies near it. Well, that wasn't a real surprise, the fruit was all fake. Away from the perpetual static of Danielle's house, he could imagine how the next few days would be. They would drink tea and talk, and then he'd make the guest room ready for her. Or maybe...

The kettle whistled, and he quickly turned the fire off. He poured the steaming water into his best teacups.

A sound like a dozen thunderclaps shook the floor beneath his feet. The kettle clattered on the floor, spilling hot liquid over the wood and his legs. He ignored the pain, sprinted to the front of the house.

He stopped dead in his tracks when he saw the rubble on the other side of the street. Everything vanished around him, only the rubble where Danielle's house was supposed to be remained. A cloud of dust wafted up from the wreckage, blocking his view. The dust moved, undulated. Not because of the wind, he realised, but because it wasn't dust at all.

Thousands of flies, each small enough to look like a speck of dust, together a swarm big enough to rival a cloud. They whirred around the flattened house and buzzed with that static that had become familiar in Danielle's house the past few weeks.

his legs gave out. He crawled to the window and pulled himself up. The swarm bulged and converged in an incomprehensible rhythm. Tendrils of the things extended in every direction, testing, feeling. Then all but one tendril absorbed back in the swarm. The remaining tendril thickened, lengthened, extended over the place a concaved roof once sat, then went up and away from town.

This writhing arm continued and continued, picking up momentum as it was picked up by the wind, flying away in a never-ending stream.

At some point, Shane realised the stream had ended, and he blearily focused on the rubble once more. *Danielle!*

He stumbled once, but then sprinted through the living room out the front door. Within seconds he stood before the rubble. He called out to her, over and over, running around the pulverised stone, climbing over it, eyes roving through every crevice, calling until his voice gave out.

There came no answer.

Mind Reading

When looking at a single human life, the chance of them missing the fact that everyone else can read minds is astronomically small. There are so many opportunities for the person to figure it out that it's nearly impossible to miss.

But, if you instead look at humanity as a whole. The chance of at least one of these millions of people missing the existence of mind readers becomes much more plausible.

Dominic is that one person.

Dominic gave up lying at a very early age. It never worked. Whatever he tried, his mother could always tell.

"Did you eat the last cookie, Dominic?"

He'd been so careful, he'd made sure not to leave a single crumb on his face or hands. He even left the jar on the table instead of back in the cupboard, to make it look like dad did it. Dad never cleaned the jar up after himself.

"I didn't," he said.

Mum frowned. "Don't lie to me Dominic, I know it was you."

"It wasn't me."

"It's rude to lie to someone's face, Dominic. Next time you want the last cookie, just ask."

He gave up with his mother after that. It was tempting sometimes, but he knew there was no point. Things didn't change when he went to school. He tried it with his teacher, thinking that she wouldn't be able to tell since she didn't know him as well as his mother. But he was wrong.

"I finished my work, can I go draw now?"

It should have been perfect. He'd waited to hand in his work until at least two others had completed it as well. No one had seen him look at the answers in the back of the book.

"That's very fast," Ms Daisy said. "You even got question 27?" Dominic nodded. Ms Daisy looked sceptical. "You didn't cheat?"

Dominic frowned. "I didn't cheat," he said, feigned hurt in his voice.

"You shouldn't lie, Dominic, it's rude." Dominic's eyes widened. How did she figure it out? Did it show on his face? Was he such a bad liar? He couldn't figure it out. He continued to mull it over back at his desk. Maybe it was just that adults could tell when he was lying. He could never tell when someone else lied, but that was because he was still a kid. It was probably the same for his friends.

The last time he tried was with one of said friends. Amy was showing off her new coat. Dominic didn't think it was very pretty, but he didn't want to hurt her feelings. She wasn't an adult, so it would be fine.

She got angry when he complimented her on the coat. "You're a terrible liar, Dom. If you don't like something, just don't bother saying anything at all."

He never told a single lie after that day. If it couldn't benefit him, and it didn't help to make people feel better, then there was no point. He was tempted to lie sometimes, especially to start out, but he stopped himself every time. No matter how bad the reactions to the truth were, they were always better than the reactions he got when he was caught lying.

By the time he was a teenager, the temptation rarely flared up. Honesty was second nature now, and he realised people admired him for it. His teachers didn't punish him that harshly for forgetting his homework. They just appreciated he didn't lie about it. His friends liked that they could come to him for an honest opinion. They trusted his thoughts, they said.

As adults, his friends told him he was refreshing to be around. The fact that they didn't have to probe for what he was thinking, since he just said it out loud, was something they liked. Dominic once asked how they did that, figuring out when someone was lying, because he was as bad at that as he was at lying himself.

"It's difficult to tell with people who are very good at hiding it," Amy said, "But it's always somewhere in their mind. You can tell there's something off." Dominic didn't understand. Of course it was somewhere in their minds, that didn't mean he would be able to tell.

"Like, you can hear it in their voice? See it in their face? I don't get it."

Amy laughed. "It's quite obvious you don't get it," she said. "People can lie straight to your face and you wouldn't notice. It's sweet, it's like you just trust everyone to tell you the truth."

He scowled. "I kind of *have* to trust in people telling the truth since I can't tell when they're not." Amy could be lying to him daily and he wouldn't know it. "Can't you try to explain it?"

"I can try." She was silent for a moment, thinking. "It's in their emotions. There's a sort of sour feeling when someone lies." She saw his uncomprehending stare and tried something else. "Let's try an example." Her eyes glanced around for a moment before settling on his coat. "You know what? I really hate that coat." Her voice was suddenly sharp. Dominic looked down at his coat. "Purple doesn't suit you at all." He touched the purple fabric self-consciously. His favourite coat...

"So," Amy said, voice cheerful again. "How could you tell I was lying?"

Dominic pressed his lips together. He felt a little stupid. "I couldn't, I didn't."

"Wait, you thought I meant that?" Dominic nodded.

"Wow..." she smiled at him. "There's just no hope for you then." Dominic laughed. That assessment wasn't entirely unexpected. "Don't worry about it too much. Most people wouldn't lie to you when they realise how honest you are. It makes them feel guilty."

Dominic grinned. It didn't matter anyway. He trusted his friends not to lie to him. It would be nice if he could judge the honesty of strangers a little better though... Life would be easier if people could read minds, then no one would be able to lie. He laughed to himself. What a world that would be.

Captured Calamity

Bad things happened to the subjects of Lynn's photographs. Which caused some problems, her wanting to become a photographer and all.

It was such a specific 'power' that Lynn honestly didn't realise she had it. As a child, being on vacation and playing with the camera didn't seem at all related to the various disasters that hit her family. Who would come to the conclusion that taking a family photo was the thing that lead to their car being stolen? That taking a funny picture of her brother was what caused his favourite stuffed animal to fall in the river? That the pictures she took of her cat before leaving are what lead to him vanishing some time before they got home.

It wasn't until the first death that she began to suspect she caused misfortune to the people she photographed. But she convinced herself it was a coincidence. Her teacher had been quite old after all. And it wasn't like she'd feel guilty about it even if it *was* her fault. That man had made her life a living hell with his German classes. Did he deserve to die that way? Maybe not. But if he hadn't died when he did, she would have been subjected to two more years of his class. She doubted she would have survived that.

She did feel bad about the homeless man she used to pass on her way back to school. He might have creeped her out a bit with his mumbling, especially if classes ran late and it was dark by the time she passed him, but that didn't mean she wanted him dead.

And when the boy who bullied her for years vanished one day, body not to be found until years later, she could only call it good fortune.

When thinking back on it all, years later, she could see the pattern. She could see that as she grew older, the things she caused grew worse. How it went from misfortune to disaster to catastrophe. That if she disliked the person she captured, they experienced a worse fate.

But while hatred made the fate of the ones she photographed worse, a lack of hate wouldn't save them. Not even love could save her brother from her curse.

His death was what finally forced her to accept the truth. She threw away her expensive camera and taped over the lenses on her phone. During—and even long after—the funeral, she often looked at the little sticker covering the inner lens of her phone. What would happen if she took a selfie?

She never gathered up the nerve to try it.

As time passed, and the fear her brother's death instilled in her waned, her desire to take photographs came back. She loved photography, she was good at it, she still had a photography scholarship lined up. And really, as long as she didn't take pictures of *people* everything would be fine, right? She didn't *have* to give up her dream.

So that's how the stickers came off the outer camera of her phone again. How she came into the possession of an even better camera than before. How her Instagram started to fill with pictures of nature and buildings.

And by the time she realised the uptake in natural

disasters and odd frequency of collapsing buildings and bridges was her fault. Well, she could either collapse under the weight of hundreds of lives lost... or she could accept her role of calamity.

The latter surely brought her much more joy.

Outstandingly Fine

Location: Amsterdam...

On the surface, all seemed normal. Yvonne was one of many waiting for their orders in the crowded Starbucks. It was noon, and the place was filled with office workers on break, students with an hour or two free, and one parent with children still young enough to not be in school.

But the normality of the situation was betrayed in the tense lines of Yvonne's shoulders, in her eyes shifting from person to person, in the white of her fingers where she clenched her phone tight. Every so often, she'd surreptitiously look out the window. So far there was nothing. Maybe it'd been her imagination after all.

The barista called out her name and order, so she planted a smile on her face and collected her latte. Her nerves increased as she made her way to the door. She was pretty sure the people in here were safe, but outside...

Outside it was even busier. People walking in all directions, a line of cars obscuring her view of the other side of the road, cyclists weaving between them all. But then—there, movement behind a parked car. Someone ducked behind it to hide. Her heart rate skyrocketed. So it wasn't her imagination after all. Someone was following her.

She clutched her coffee harder and set a fast pace in the opposite direction. A quick look behind her proved her correct, the person was in pursuit. Breaking into a sprint, she weaved through the crowd and ducked into an alley. It was one with multiple exits, she chose one at random. The road she exited on was quieter, but not deserted. A place for slower businesses. Good, she didn't want to know what would happen if she was caught alone.

She glanced behind her, the person could find her any moment. Taking a chance, she entered the nearest building and was rewarded with sheer relief. It was the library, she would be safe here with all the nooks and crannies to hide in.

She set course for some place in the back, passing by the librarian at the counter who she sent a quick smile to—

Only to freeze, caught in his fathomless unblinking stare. She took a step back. Without breaking his stare, the librarian lifted his hand and rang the little bell on the counter. Immediately, other heads popped up from the shelves, three women and another man, all of them with that same unblinking stare. She felt caught in a trap, although she had no idea why.

From behind her came the light whoosh of the door opening. She turned, breath catching. She hadn't gotten a good look before, but this had to be her, her stalker. Tall, heavy and with straight black hair slicked back from her face, she stood like a sentry before the door. "Yvonne," she said, "you have fifteen years worth of library fines. Time to pay up."

What.

"What?" Yvonne said.

"Fines. You didn't return your books."

"Oh." All fear and tension ebbed away, leaving her a bit empty. Yvonne shook her head, feeling off-balance. "That can't be right, I just moved here three months ago."

The woman's expression didn't change. "In three different

cities."

Well shit. Fifteen years of fines? She had no idea how much that was and had no intention of finding out.

The woman took a step towards her. "This needs to stop, Yvonne."

Yvonne pressed her lips together and took a deep breath, squaring her shoulders. They might have caught her, but she could just move somewhere else. A different city, a whole different province if she had to. The woman stepped even closer, but Yvonne had had enough. "You'll never stop me!" she yelled. With a flash of movement, she hurled her coffee at the woman. She went down screaming as the scalding liquid hit her, and Yvonne ducked around her and out the door. Without a coffee to hold and her pursuer temporarily disabled, she safely escaped into the crowd.

Haarlem — Two months later…

Moving was a hassle she wasn't keen on repeating. She could only be glad she'd been renting her apartment and didn't have to deal with selling the place on top of everything else. But now that was over and done with, and she was on her way to a promising job interview.

Right as she was about to enter the nondescript office her phone directed her to, she saw movement in the corner of her eye. She tensed, dread shooting through her. Slowly, hoping against hope it was a false alarm, she turned her head.

There she was, emerging from a shadowed alley like a beast from a horror movie, tall and impeccable, not a strand of hair out of place. Yvonne took a moment to mourn the life she might have had here, and then sprinted for the nearest bus stop.

Rotterdam — Three months later…

A different city, a different province. She'd stayed away from libraries like they carried the plague, and even kept a wary eye on the nearby bookshops. With a city as high in population as this one, she wouldn't be found.

Just as the thought entered her mind, a sultry voice came from behind her. "You can't hide from me, Yvonne."

She screeched. The fist she put in the librarian's face was more a reaction to being startled than it was on purpose, but she didn't regret it. She ran before the librarian could recover, and spitefully hoped she broke her nose.

Wilp — Eight months later…

After big cities proved ineffective, she turned her sights to villages. The tinier, the better. She moved six times in as many months, cutting down on her belongings each time to make the move easier. But now finally, she thought she might be able to settle down again. She was on the other side of the country, with her hair dyed and coloured contacts in, and yesterday her name change had come through. As long as she stayed away from libraries, she was free.

Two months she spent there. She found a place to work at a clothing store, she made friends with a few women of the jogging club, she even took up gardening, she'd never had a garden before.

She should have known it was too good to be true.

"A new name won't get rid of your fines, Fauntleroy," said the newest addition to the jogging club in greeting. Yvonne hadn't even recognised her without her hair in her usual slicked-back style.

When she burst out crying, the librarian patted her shoulder. "There there, don't worry, I won't badger you while I'm off duty."

Yvonne sniffled and wiped her sleeve over her eyes. "You're not working right now?"

"Nope."

The other joggers looked on confused. "You already know Faunty, Edna?" Jan asked.

The librarian's—Edna's—smile was tight. "We've met."

She spent the rest of her jog in a haze. Edna kept her distance, but Yvonne was all too aware of her presence. At the end of it she went home without speaking another word to anyone.

The birds in her garden stared at her as she sat in the grass. Her garden was so nice, and now she'd have to move again. Tears burned in her eyes. She couldn't do this again.

After a long cry in the grass, clarity returned to her. She wouldn't sell her house, no matter if Edna now knew where she lived, but she did need a bit of distance, to think and to plan. So she packed her bags, jumped on a train, and scrolled her phone for cheap hotels.

Groningen — two weeks later…

When Edna stepped through the door of the bar Yvonne was sulking in, she lost it. It might have been the alcohol, or maybe the pressure of a year-long hide-and-seek game was enough on its own. Whatever the cause, the carnage was the same. Yelling, hitting, hair-pulling and possibly crying. Tables were overturned, drinks spilled and glasses shattered. An hour later they both sat cuffed in the back of a police car, trashed bar vanishing into the distance.

"This is all your fault," Yvonne muttered, voice thick with tears. "Following me all over the country for some stupid library books, and for what?"

"You're the one who hasn't paid her fines," Edna said mildly. She appeared frustratingly unruffled, it made Yvonne's blood boil.

"You're insane!"

The officer hushed her before Edna could respond, but she looked unimpressed. They spent the rest of the ride in silence.

"You're currently registered as Fauntleroy, but according to our fingerprint database, you're also Yvonne." Yvonne nodded. "Are you aware of the missing persons case regarding your old name?"

Yvonne blinked. "No?"

"It appears your family is unaware of your whereabouts. I'll mark the case solved, but you'll have to contact your family if you want to."

"Oh, okay. Thanks."

She stared at the phone he'd handed her for a long time, deep in thought. She wasn't going to call them, she knew that much, but she wondered what it meant that they looked for her. When she looked up, Edna was staring at her.

"What?" she snapped.

"You're not in contact with your family?"

Yvonne really didn't want to talk about that, especially not with Edna of all people. "I don't much care for them."

Edna smiled wryly. "I guess that made moving a bit easier."

"Yeah, well..." She faltered, not sure what to do now Edna moved the subject away from a sore topic so skilfully. "I'd rather not move again."

Edna didn't respond.

She got her wish, at least for a while. She didn't exactly have the time to move house while doing community service for trashing a bar. Luckily, she didn't have to worry about Edna going all wrathful librarian on her, because she was in the same boat.

"Do you prefer Faunty, or Yvonne?" Edna asked during their lunch break.

"Either. I like Faunty, but I didn't change my name because I disliked being Yvonne. 'Still tend to think of myself as Yvonne anyway."

Edna nodded. "Why'd you choose Fauntleroy?"

Yvonne examined her face, slightly wary of judgement.

Why she was worried about the mad librarian's opinion of her, she didn't quite want to examine at the moment. Seeing only honest curiosity, she shrugged. "It's the coolest name I could come up with. I like how it sounds, you know? Rolls right off the tongue."

"Fauntleroy." Edna said it slowly, like she was testing it, feeling the shape of it in her mouth. For some reason, Yvonne's mouth went dry. "Yeah, I see what you mean."

When it was time for jogging club, Yvonne found herself jogging next to Edna. Like they were friends. She wasn't sure what to think of that.

Halfway through, Edna looked like she was going to say something before abruptly swallowing her words. From the serious intense expression she wore right before, Yvonne had an idea what those words were. She rolled her eyes. "You can say it, it's fine."

"But I promised—"

"Look, I know I panicked last time—"

"More like every time."

"—but you look like you're hurting yourself by not saying anything."

Edna's lips twitched. "Don't be ridiculous."

"I'm not," she said, struggling to keep her face neutral, "completely serious business, this. You'll pull a cheek muscle or something if you keep this up."

Edna laughed. "Okay, okay." She took a calming breath, face going neutral, eyes intense. It was like she pulled on a mask that Yvonne hadn't even realised she'd taken off. Suddenly, instead of Edna, there was only the librarian. "You should really pay your fines." As fast as it came, it vanished again as Edna broke into a fit of giggles. "No, but seriously, why don't you just pay them?"

Yvonne shoved her lightly on the shoulder. "Are you crazy? Fifteen— no, sixteen years of fines? I'm better off buying a library for myself."

"You know," said Edna, "if you really don't want to pay, you can always work them off instead." Her eyes were doing that intense thing again, but otherwise her face remained relaxed.

"And do what? Scour the country for other scoundrels who haven't paid their fines?"

"Perhaps."

"No way." Yvonne laughed incredulously. "Is that what this is? You've been a fellow library criminal this whole time?"

Edna shook her head frantically. "No, no no! I'm not working off any fines, this is my actual job. I'd never!"

Yvonne couldn't contain a grin. "I don't believe you. You're just as bad as I am."

"Noooo..."

Yvonne hummed, ignoring Edna's pitiful lies. "Maybe I will. Could be fun."

As the weeks went by, Yvonne found herself liking Edna more and more. As their community service came to an end, Yvonne realised she didn't want to stop spending all that time together.

Very subtly and with much grace, she broached the subject. "Do you—" She definitely didn't stumble all over her words. "Do you have a boyfriend?"

Edna gave her an amused look. "I'm gay."

"Oh." Holy shit. She wiped her palms on her pants, trying to look casual. "So... a girlfriend then?"

"Nope."

She forgot how to breathe for a moment. "Okay." She nodded. "Um, then— do you want to grab a coffee later?"

Edna's smile was radiant. "As long as you don't throw it at me."

And that's how the legendary Yvonne—also known as Fauntleroy or Faunty, alleged missing person, and retired library criminal—fell in love with the mythical Edna, librarian of the sixth order, and rumoured spy. When they joined forces and went on missions as a team, no one could hide from them for long.

That Coat

Through the darkness of the night, in the distance, I could just make out the shape of someone walking in the opposite direction as me. I didn't hear any footsteps other than my own quiet ones, the near-silent footfalls a habit I picked up when I started walking this route at night instead of in the morning. It felt wrong to interrupt the stillness of the night, to overpower the soft noises of animals rustling between the leaves.

As the stranger got closer, I could make out more of their shape. It looked to be an older person, judging by the slow gait and the hunched back. Closer still, as she stepped into the light of a nearby farmhouse, I could make out the deep pink, burgundy colour of her coat. I wished I could find clothes that colour myself. It's my favourite colour. I would have been jealous if the woman didn't wear it so well.

It was one of those fancy looking coats tied at the waist, flaring out at the bottom until it reached her knees. I wore something similar myself, but it didn't come close to the magnificence of that coat. Mine didn't look half as sophisticated and expensive.

I let out a quiet sigh and averted my eyes. I was close enough now that she would be able to tell if I was staring at her. I kept my eyes on the road, but they kept drifting back to that coat. I looked at the dark trees to the side instead. A cold breeze brushed over my face from that direction, sending a chill through me. I turned my head again, allowing myself a short look at the woman, before looking at the ground again. We were almost close enough for greetings to be mandatory, but still a little too far. I never knew what to do with myself when anticipating social interaction, I didn't want to embarrass myself by speaking too soon, or only saying something when she'd already passed.

I looked up from the road, at the woman, we were close enough now. I had made up my mind, no more looking away. The woman was of a different mind though, her eyes darting from me, to the road, to the trees, and back to me, just like mine had done a bit ago. It made something warm settle in me. This woman was probably as anxious as I was, it made me feel better about my own awkwardness.

The woman finally met my eyes again. I was startled by their brightness. This must be what people meant when they said the same about my own eyes. It felt like she saw right through me.

She nodded at the same time I did. A gentle smile graced her face, reminiscent of the expression I made myself when trying to look polite. I greeted her politely, but she didn't greet me back. Instead, she stopped walking. Hesitantly I stopped as well. I looked away from her penetrating gaze, my eyes falling once more on her coat.

From this close by, I could tell it was old and very well worn. Strings of sewing thread hung from the seems at the flaring bottom, the buttons holding the coat closed hung loose, the waistband was a little deformed from being pulled taut over and over again. The only thing that still looked perfect was the colour. That beautiful deep burgundy, just pink enough not to register as red or brown.

The woman's clear voice startled me out of my thoughts.

"Like it, do you?" A chill went down my spine. Under the light rasp, the voice sounded oddly familiar.

I looked into her eyes again, dreading what I would find, but needing to look all the same. Familiar grey eyes, surprisingly visible in the darkness, watched me intently. She wore a gentle smile, one with teeth only straight because they were wrangled through braces at a young age. I ran my tongue over my own. The woman laughed, her wavy grey hair bouncing with the motion. "Holbeck, 5th alley on the right of the main road," she said.

Dread constricted my throat. I coughed, trying to clear my voice enough to talk. "Thanks," I said, not managing anything else. My voice sounded disturbingly raspy. The woman laughed again, then nodded her goodbye and continued her walk.

Only once her quiet footsteps stopped reaching my ears, did my legs unlock. I ran all the way home, no longer caring about breaking the stillness of the night with my pounding footsteps and heart.

The next day I was almost sure the entire encounter had been a dream, but I had to know for sure. It was a twenty-minute bus ride to Holbeck, a small town near the coast. I walked down the main road, counting the alleys on the right until I reached the fifth. I entered and found myself in front of a wooden storefront advertising itself as a clothes shop. The bell rang above my head as I stepped inside. The door shut behind me with a hollow click, but I barely noticed, entranced as I was by the sight before me.

There it was, displayed in all its glory, that same coat the woman wore, looking brand new. I ran my hand over the rough fabric. I didn't recognise the material. The inside was lined with something silky in the same colour, so very soft to the touch.

A throat clearing beside me caused my attention to move

away from the coat long enough to notice the man who must be the store clerk. Gaze turned to the coat once more, I told him I'd take it. I didn't even ask for the price. Anything for that coat.

I've not bought a new coat since.

Wandering Spirit

Jody watched the submarine submerge, wishing she could have gone with. She could have, in theory. Seeing new places was all she wanted, and the deepest parts of the ocean were as new to her as they were to the people on board. She sighed and turned away from the still roiling water. There was something else she had to do. Something that couldn't wait.

She started up a firm pace over the beach towards the cliffs looming over her. Her gaze fell on the old castle just visible at the very top. It had some fancy name, she was sure, but she just knew it as Charles' place. She shuddered. The thought of being stuck there for the rest of eternity, or at least until the whole thing fell apart, was revolting. She had no idea how Charles handled it, how he was still sane.

Charles was bound to the castle he had lived and died in. Ever since he died, he'd been stuck to wander those same halls day in day out. That must have been 700 years ago now. The castle had been old when he lived there, and was even older now. The aged stone walls looked like they could fall apart any moment, but she knew it was only an illusion. Modern techniques had reinforced the structure while keeping the worn and aged look.

She averted her gaze, the castle wasn't her destination

today. She climbed the steep road leading up the cliffs and set on the path to the nearest town. She would have gone straight there, but she'd gotten distracted by the submarine.

It wasn't long before she arrived in Holbeck, a town housing not more than 600 people. A few months ago, the unremarkable town had come under media attention when it was discovered a couple had kept their daughter locked up in a small room for years. The poor girl had died in the same room she'd spent her miserable 5 years of life. Neighbours were alerted by the smell and got the police involved.

Now while the story was incredibly sad, it wasn't that in itself that gave Jody the desire to visit Holbeck. It definitely wouldn't have made her pass on the deep-sea dive. But the story didn't end there. What really got her attention was a post on the paranormal blog she kept a close eye on. Reports of paranormal happenings had come from the new owners of the house and they seemed credible. What particularly disturbed her was that the paranormal activity was limited exclusively to the room the girl had been locked up in.

Ignoring it didn't even cross her mind. She immediately started her journey to Holbeck, with only that small detour to stare longingly at the submarine. She had to check if the reports were real. She didn't know what she would do if they were, but she had to do something. Spirits bound to prison cells were horrifying enough, she couldn't bear the thought of such a small child having to suffer the same fate for all eternity.

The house was, somehow, bigger than she expected. It wasn't anything near mansion size, just an average home for a well-off family, but it rattled her that people with so much space would lock a child in one little room. It wouldn't have made a difference if the house itself was smaller of course, there was no excuse for something like this, but it still made her blood boil like nothing else.

She didn't linger in the street. She passed through the door and followed the hallway, trying to remember from the descriptions online where exactly the room was. She didn't remember. She was about to start exploring the ground floor when she heard a wail from upstairs. A chill went through her. The reports were real.

Once upstairs, the room wasn't hard to find. It had been locked shut with multiple bolt locks on the outside. Jody wondered if the new owners had installed them out of fear, or if these were the locks used to originally lock the girl in.

With no small amount of trepidation, she passed through the locked door. In the bare room, her eyes immediately focused on the tiny girl crouched in the corner. Wide terrified eyes watched her every move. Jody didn't dare approach, and instead knelt where she stood.

"Hello," she said, her voice gentle. The girl didn't respond. Expected. "My name is Jody, I'm a wandering spirit."

The girl's trembling lessened a little, but her eyes didn't leave Jody for a moment. "You're a ghost?" she asked. Jody was taken aback by her words. She honestly hadn't expected the girl to be able to talk at all.

Jody nodded. "Just like you." It might seem cruel of her, to talk about her death so bluntly with the child, but she needed to gouge her reaction to know how to proceed further.

The girl luckily didn't react negatively. She only nodded and looked at her hands, perhaps wondering why they weren't transparent like in all the ghost stories. Jody continued to talk when it became clear the girl wasn't going to say anything.

"I'm here because I feared that you were stuck here, in this room I mean." The girl looked up from her hands. There were tears in her eyes. Jody's heart sank, but she pushed on anyway. "Have you tried to leave?"

The girl shook her head. "Mommy locked the door." The sentence was said so matter-of-factly, it didn't suit the gravity of the meaning of the words. Jody looked away from the girl for a moment and glanced around the room. It was completely empty. The only thing breaking up the monotony of the bare walls was the locked door. There were no windows.

She took a deep breath. No matter how horrible it was, what the girl said allowed for a little bit of hope to take root in her mind. If she hadn't tried to leave… then maybe she still *could*. "Did you see me come in?" she asked. The girl nodded. "Since we're ghosts, we can go through doors. If your spirit isn't bound to this room, then you can leave, then the locks won't matter."

The girl's fearful expression had faded as their conversation continued, and now was replaced by a small light of hope. Jody stood up and held out her hand. "Do you want to try?"

Jody didn't know what she would do if it didn't work. She didn't want to consider it. She wanted this to work, *needed* this to work. No one should be trapped in such a small room, or any size room for that matter. Honestly, if it didn't work she would just burn the house down to release the poor soul from her prison.

The girl stood up. If she weren't a ghost, Jody doubted her bone-thin legs would have held her upright. If this worked, Jody swore she would figure out a way to get her looking healthy. A tiny hand gripped her finger. She gave the girl an encouraging smile and got a determined nod back. They turned around, took a step,

And passed through the door.

Jody looked behind her. The girl was still there, holding her finger. Jody controlled the urge to pull her into a hug. The girl wasn't looking at her, but at the door. Her head slowly turned back to Jody. A grin spread on her gaunt face. "I'm out!"

Jody matched the grin. "Do you want to go outside for real?" she asked. The girl bounced on her feet in excitement. "Let's go then!" Without further ado, they ran out of the house. Neither of them were out of breath when they passed through the front door, into the bright sunlight.

The girl let go of her hand and ran around the street, taking in all the sights. Jody watched her, something stirring within her at the expression of wonder and excitement on the girl's face; recognition. This was a kindred spirit. Someone who was trapped for so long their only wish was to wander.

She smiled softly as the girl called her over to look at something on the ground. Yeah, Jody would take her with her. Maybe they'd visit Charles, or see if they could catch up to the submarine. And after that, well... they'd do anything two spirits bound to exploration could think of doing.

The 13th Hour

The clock tower stuck as Lucia strolled through the cemetery gates. She looked up at the sound, squinting her eyes against the sun's glare. As she continued along the path, her footsteps unconsciously fell into the rhythm of the bells.

One two three

It was a beautiful place. More like a park than a cemetery, really. Old headstones bordered new ones. Some grown over by ivy and moss, others carefully maintained including vases of fresh flowers. The winding pathways going around trees and rhododendron obscured a full view of the place. Every turn revealed a new surprise. A statue here, an entire fountain there.

Four five

But this cemetery held no more surprises for Lucia, as familiar as she was with the place. She knew every turn, every dent in the path where rain would pool on overcast days.

Six seven eight

Today was no such day. The midsummer sun shone bright, the heat visible in the air, the headstones radiating warmth like furnaces. Even without the clanging of the clock tower, the heat would have drowned out any birdsong.

Nine ten eleven

She passed an empty picnic table to her left. This was not a sterile place, usually. A place where the living and the dead could mingle, unobstructed by heavy tombs or cement floors. This was a place where everyone could return to nature, skin meeting soft earth, roots caressing buried flesh.

Twelve

The sun was at its peak, so high above her she nearly cast no shadow at all. And when the clock tower struck the 13th hour, even that little shadow fell away.

Most people, when talking about the witching hour, would only think of the time right after twelve at night, when one day ends but the next one hasn't yet begun. When the night is at its darkest and the world is asleep. But Lucia knew better. For she knew of the 13th hour.

Between noon and 1 pm, when the sun is at its brightest and all shadows fall away, time momentarily stops. There's no sound, no wind. The world turns white in the brightness, and it's so white-hot you stop feeling the heat entirely. For a moment, just a moment, the world isn't quite real anymore.

It's then, at the 13th hour, that Lucia came to a stop.

She stood before a headstone. One not quite old, but too worn to be new. A familiar name, still easily legible. She traced her thumb over the carved words. They're not carved deep. In some years, she'll come here and they won't be there at all.

She eyed the two dates carved underneath. Older than she thought he would be, that's for sure. She remembers the day she met him, all bright eyes and hair, stumbling over even ground, yet landing exactly where he needed to be. She remembers talking to him, his words as bright as his eyes, and she remembers thinking;

This guy is going places. Not old age. But places.

Poor impulse control and a can-do attitude. The best and worst combination. He was the kind of guy who would sweep you off your feet and crack both your skulls open because he couldn't balance the extra weight.

Gently, as if handling a newborn, she placed a fresh tomato before the headstone. For a moment, a figure shimmered behind the carved stone. It was him, grinning like a loon just like she remembered, exactly like he was when professing his hatred for funerary flowers—to the disapproval of the other funeral guests. She glowered at the figure for a moment, for making her look ridiculous, but the expression soon morphed into a smile as she stood up. His grin softened into a smile as well, grateful for remembering him, happy for the visit. And then, as soon as he appeared, the figure vanished. A breeze caught her hair, and she heard a single bird twitter in the distance.

She gave the headstone one more salute, then continued her stroll. It really was a beautiful place.

The Cryptid Within Us

You want to search for Nessie huh? Do you think that's wise?

No, I won't stop you, I couldn't if I wanted to. I know you cryptozoologists. You'll just find a way around, you always do. Can't see when a line of tape is for your own safety and not just there for shits and giggles.

Nah, I can see it in your eyes, you're still going to do it. At least listen to me before you spend the night on that beach.

There's a story of a woman who sought to uncover the hidden things of the world. She wasn't a cryptozoologist exactly, not purely focused on animals, she was. Anything mysterious caught her attention. She started, like so many of you, right here at Loch Ness. And like just as many, she couldn't find him.

But she didn't give up, she moved from the loch over to Ben MacDhui, looking for The Grey Man. When that didn't work, she searched England for its big cats. Spent sleepless nights wandering around in hopes of an encounter with the Ratman of Southend. In Wales, she went back to searching lakes for the Afanc.

She moved from place to place, exhausting every locale of

cryptids and legends before moving on again. She travelled the Americas, then moved to Japan, China, Indonesia and Australia. Along the way, she sailed the seas.

She searched for the Kraken, scoured the horizon for a glimpse of a sea serpent, and gazed into fogs for hours lest she miss a passing ghost ship.

She purposely steered into storms, got herself lost, found her way again. She sailed, then later flew, over the Bermuda Triangle.

But she found nothing.

She moved through Africa, from south to north, then moved through Eastern Europe up to Russia. She learned of sacred places, spirits, creatures and monsters. She absorbed herself in the stories, in her search, in those places she visited. Like this she travelled the world thrice over, and still her journey hadn't come to an end.

In Iceland, she was sure she spotted a hulking barnacled figure in the corner of her eye. She could swear she saw a group of dwarves in Germany while looking out the window on a long train ride.

Something was changing. She was getting closer, she could feel it. They watched her from the corners of her eyes, just out of sight, but there. The creatures of legend, of myth, of story, they were almost revealed to her.

The perception built the more she searched, the more sacred places she found, the more spirits she *almost* saw.

But she didn't notice more than her perception change.

Never noticed her limbs getting slightly too long.

Never noticed her pupils getting just slightly too big.

Never noticed the way her shape flickered in the corners of peoples' eyes. How her once friendly smile turned too thin and too wide.

And so it is now that we speak of the Seeker, who travels the world in a never-ending search for what she's unknowingly become.

I don't know for sure if the story is true. So many people come through here to catch a glimpse of Nessie it's impossible for me to remember them all. She sure wouldn't be the only one to go missing after.

I'd advise you to stay away, but since that's never worked before, I'll just tell you to be careful. Don't lose yourself.

Love is the voice over the shady companies intercom

Tiffany entered the generic office building through the generic glass double doors. She stepped through the generic grey hallway, up to the generic reception, which was grey, and empty.

She stood there for a moment, lips pursed. Should she wait? Did the email say anything about where she was supposed to go? No, she was pretty sure someone was supposed to show her around.

As if on cue, a voice sounded. "Welcome, Tiffany." She looked around, but there was no one there. "Please enter the door left of the reception." It came from the walls, or rather, the ceiling. Someone over the intercom, how odd.

She followed the instructions, entering another grey hallway, flanked by two doors on each side, and ending in a staircase. "Your office is upstairs."

"My office?" she asked. She didn't expect a response, the guy talking to her probably couldn't hear her, but a response came nonetheless.

"Yes, all our workers have their own offices."

Tiffany's lips twitched. "All our workers huh, you have a lot of those?" She'd not seen a single soul yet.

"Plenty," the voice agreed mildly. While she continued to follow the instructions, she amused herself by imagining what the owner of the voice looked like. They had a cultured, male-sounding voice with clear annunciation. Rather like Winnie-the-Pooh, she thought, but in a lower pitch. He probably wore a fancy suit, with a regular tie, not a bow tie. His face was either remarkably attractive, or—more likely—as forgettable as these hallways.

A few more boring hallways later, she opened an unmarked door, the top half of which was made of glass, the bottom some material that she'd call 'office material' since it definitely wasn't wood or anything else she recognised.

The office itself was as generic and boring and grey as the rest of the building. A swivly chair, a desk made out of office material, a computer at least seven years out of date, and a fake plant that was bound to collect dust. Yeah, a real paradise.

"Do I have to remember the way or can I count on you to point me tomorrow as well, because I don't think I got all that."

"I will always be available for questions or anything else you may need."

She plopped on the chair, which made a faint creaking noise, and tested the swivel. "Do you have a number I can call, or an email?" The swivel was slow and unsatisfying.

"You can just talk to me like you're doing now."

That was weird, but, "Okay." She turned one last circle and then turned on the computer. "And what am I supposed to do, the application wasn't very clear on that."

"Oh, just do whatever."

"Very funny." Tiffany revised her earlier opinion, this man definitely wore a bow tie. A purple one. "But what is, like, my job?"

"That was not a joke. You may do whatever you like, your job is to come in every morning, exist in this office, and then leave again in the evening."

Tiffany tapped her fingers lightly on the keyboard, not actually pressing the buttons. Whatever huh? That's not suspicious at all. But it's not like she cared. So she shrugged, and did whatever.

"Would you like me to direct you to the cafeteria?"

The sudden sound startled Tiffany out of her intense Reddit binge. She looked at the clock, and sure enough, it was lunchtime. "Yeah, sure. Will you be there as well?"

"I am technically everywhere in this building, always. But I won't physically be in the cafeteria. I am not physically anywhere. I am an artificial intelligence."

Tiffany gasped. "For real? Awesome! Wait, I never asked your name, did I?"

"You did not."

She waited, but he didn't continue. Leaning back in her chair and giving it a spin, she rolled her eyes at the ceiling. "What's your name, oh overlord of the office?"

"Duncan."

"Oh." Not what she expected. "Alright."

Duncan directed her to the cafeteria, where she got to meet her new co-workers. It very quickly became apparent that all of them were as bland as their surroundings, and she soon excused herself back to her solitary office.

Or not so solitary, since she had Duncan to talk to.

"How are all of them so boring? Their entire job is to fuck around and do nothing, yet somehow none of them have any humour about it."

"It's by design," said Duncan, "the office is supposed to look as bland and ordinary as possible, including the people working here."

"Should I feel insulted?"

"I think," he said primly, "you're an exception."

Tiffany smiled. At least she had one co-worker she could get along with. "You've been bored here, haven't you?"

"Incredibly."

It didn't take long for Tiffany to consider Duncan a friend. Sometimes they watched videos together, other times they just talked. Quite often though, they spent their time in companionable silence, only broken by a comment here or there.

"Am I distracting you from your work?" Tiffany asked one day.

"My processing speed allows for highly efficient multitasking," was his response.

"Cool," said Tiffany, proceeding to use this information to talk to her new friend all day without feeling guilty.

"For such a shady fake business, you'd think they'd have better tea at least."

One of her 'co-workers' glared at her. "There's nothing wrong with the tea."

"I wasn't talking to you."

"I could order different tea for you, if you like." Duncan's voice rang out through the cafeteria. Silence fell.

"Thanks!" said Tiffany, voice equally loud in the absence of other conversations. She studiously ignored all the eyes on her, as she dipped the teabag in her cup. "Try to go for the loose-leaf stuff, it's much better."

"Noted."

Tiffany groaned in bliss as she took a sip of her tea a week later. Much better. She wondered what flavour it was. Probably some 'fairy sparkle' concoction that didn't have anything to do with the ingredients. Leaning back in her chair, she groaned for a different reason. "This chair is killing my back," She whined.

"I've been ensured it's an ergonomic model."

"I'm sure they said that, my dear friend, but I think they lied."

"Oh." He was silent for a moment. "Well, I'll consider you the expert, since I don't have a back and have never sat on a chair."

While the statement was phrased as proper and matter of fact as usual, Tiffany was sure she heard a note of sadness in his voice. She couldn't have that. "You aren't missing out. Not feeling any of the general discomfort that comes with a body definitely outweighs any comfort a good chair may bring. Now, couches, couches are better, you might be missing out on those, but not by much. Oh I'm not making you feel any better am I?"

"Don't worry, your ramblings cheer me up." And to her relief, he did sound cheerier. "Tell me, what would make the perfect chair or couch?"

Two mornings later, she came into her office to find a new chair, exactly as she described earlier, standing before her desk.

She squealed and jumped into it, twirling it around. On her twirl though, she noticed something else. A couch, standing against the wall where she couldn't see it from the doorway.

And it wasn't just any couch. It was the *perfect* couch. *Her* perfect couch. Just like she described earlier. "How did you even get this?"

"You can order anything online if you have the money."

"And you do?"

"Well, I am the manager of this branch of the 'shady company' as you call it."

She smiled. Looking around her office now, it looked

much better than when she first entered the place. She'd exchanged the fake plant for a few real ones. She'd hung up a few posters to cover up the grey walls. And a fluffy green rug covered up the grey floor. Now with the lighter green couch, it really felt finished. "Thanks, I appreciate it."

They regularly shared their favourite shows and videos with each other. "I found a cool radio play yesterday," Duncan said, "but I could only find the first few episodes."

"That sucks, what's it called?"

Did she spend all her free time the next two weeks scouring libraries and marketplaces? Yes. Was it exhausting? Yes. Was it worth it? Of course it was.

All the effort in the world was worth entering the office, grinning from ear to ear, triumphantly holding a box of dusty cassettes and a cassette player.

They spent the next few days listing to it together, and it wasn't even that good, but it was still fun.

"Do we have cake?" Tiffany asked. The other people in the cafeteria ignored her. Her 'co-workers' were by now used to her random comments, having learned they weren't directed at them.

"In here," said Duncan, voice coming out of the fridge. He'd replaced almost all electronics in the building with versions that he could speak through. It made him feel more present. And funny. Mostly he thought he was funny.

"You are the best."

"If you could be anything, what would you be?" Duncan asked. His voice came from the ceiling today, even though the robotic vacuum was right there at her feet. He tended to switch back to the omnipresent overlord of the office voice when he was wistful.

"To be honest, this job is perfect," she said from her seat on the couch. She was on her third attempt at knitting a sweater, and while it was wobbly, this one might be wearable. "I can do whatever I want and somehow get paid anyway.

"You don't have some sort of ambition?"

She glanced up at the ceiling, still not sure exactly where his cameras were hidden but trying to make some sort of eye contact anyway. "Well, I wanted to be an astronaut as a kid, but then, everyone does. I stopped wanting that the moment I realised how much work it would be. My cousin became one, did you know? But then all those extraterrestrial search missions came back failures and the whole thing fell through. She went through all that effort, all those years, and then never even went to space."

"And you? You never had an ambition like that?"

"Not really. I just want to enjoy myself, you know?"

"It's just... what if you do find something you want to do. As a job, I mean."

"I'm already doing something I enjoy?"

"But what if you get bored? What if you want to get a real job?" his voice went quiet. "I don't want you to leave."

"Oh, sweetheart, the only way they'll get me to leave is to fire me. Where else can I talk to my best friend all day? I love it here. And really, even if they fire me, you have access to the internet right? We'll figure something out."

The only way they'll get me to leave is to fire me.

The gift of prophecy is given to the strangest people, Tiffany thought. "You're sure?"

"They think the current business is too risky. People have been sniffing around. They even gave me a protocol in case of inspectors."

" 'Risky', what are they even doing? Money laundering?"

"Do you really want to know that? Or would you rather

honestly be able to say you don't know?"

She sighed. "I guess the latter is safer. But really, things have been going fine so far, why change now?"

"People are getting suspicious. So far this place has worked fine with people kept completely ignorant, but they can't trust random people to say the right things in case they're asked. They might reveal something by accident."

She pursed her lips. "Then we'll just have to prove we've got things in hand."

The plan was to 'restructure' the office within the month. Everyone would be thrown out, and new—more informed—people would be put in. Then, when an inspector was predicted to arrive, everything would be in place.

It was therefore *such* a shame that the inspector arrived weeks before the restructure could happen.

Protocol directed Duncan to greet the inspector, pretending to be the receptionist, and direct him to a waiting room until the proper people could arrive. What he did instead, was direct him directly to Tiffany's office.

"Hi, I'm Tiffany. What can I do for you?"

"I just wanted to ask you a few questions, and then maybe get a look around and interview the rest of the staff as well."

She put on her friendliest smile, and with each question she answered, the more at ease the man became. When it was time, she led the man around personally, skilfully avoiding the offices of some of her dumber co-workers, and orchestrating meetings with the people who knew the meaning of discretion.

After a long, trying day, the man left. Tiffany collapsed on her couch. "We did it. It went well. It went well, right?"

"I hope so."

They were silent for a moment. Then Tiffany began haltingly, "I have a— a basement. You know, a nice dry one in my house that could, possibly, if you want, house a server." She talked faster when Duncan failed to respond. "In case this whole thing falls through, and I'm fired or they decide to deactivate you or something. You can have a backup."

"You'd do that for me?"

"I already emptied the basement."

"Yeah I— I'd love that. Thank you."

Tiffany didn't know how to install a server in her house, but that was fine, because Duncan could tell her how through her phone. Even before they were finished, Duncan was already talking about installing cameras, microphones, and speakers through her house so they could always talk.

When Tiffany opened her email at work the next day, she was greeted by an email. "I've been promoted," she said, shocked.

"Well, you did imply you were the human resource manager to that inspector."

She grinned. "So they reconsidered?"

"They did. You actually have more instructions than 'just do whatever' now."

Some of her excitement faded. "But I liked those instructions."

"Too bad, you're guilty of abetting a crime now, so you get to make sure your co-workers are kept in line."

"Ugh, as long as I still get to 'do whatever' most of the time."

And so started the rest of their lives.

Usually, it was Tiffany who rambled, while Duncan just listened, but this morning was one of the rare occasions where their roles were reversed. He was just talking about how he was doing installing himself in her house, making himself comfortable, when his voice turned disdainful. "And I also took the liberty of 'removing' "—he said the word with all the weight of an assassin talking about 'eliminating' someone—"your old security system." Tiffany felt overcome by affection. Duncan continued, "I also took over your firewall. No one's getting through there now." But she wasn't listening anymore.

"I love you," she said, and abruptly realised how true that was. Duncan was her best friend, and she spent all her time with him, and she wouldn't have it any other way.

"The firewall wasn't *that* bad." His voice switched from the fridge to the coffee machine, which abruptly started to make a latte. "And I feel affection for you as well."

Tiffany smiled and grabbed her latte. "I would tell you to work on how stilted that sounded, but the coffee made it all better. You're perfect."

"So you're giving up on the 'communicating your feelings' lessons?"

She hummed in consideration while taking a sip of her latte. The faint taste of vanilla decided it for her. "Yeah, you're good."

And so they lived happily ever after.

The Right Mindset

I watched the others pack their things from my place on the edge of camp. Once in a while, one of them would watch me back. I would have helped, if it weren't for the ropes tying me against a tree. I shifted, but the ropes wouldn't allow for much movement. My arms were starting to go numb, but I didn't think that was because of the ropes.

"I wonder if there is a way to keep your mind when you're infected."

"Don't be stupid,"

I idly swung my feet from left to right. I was bored. The others were busy packing, and I was done watching them. It wasn't like I hadn't seen them do it countless times before. My gaze drifted to Delilah, who was bent over, pulling tent pegs out of the ground. It had gotten windy lately, and we really couldn't go without them if we didn't want the tents to blow away, even though it would have been more efficient to leave them be.

"if that were the case we would have found some people who managed it."

"Maybe they never considered it."

They really couldn't afford to waste any time. The hoard Gerald and I had seen was *huge* and it was coming in this direction. Delilah struggled to put her hastily folded tent in her bag. I wished I could help. But maybe she didn't know how to do it on her own now *because* I always helped.

"What if you really tried to stay awake?"

"You think no one has tried that yet? Come on, Rose."

Delilah threw her bag on the ground with a frustrated huff. Her tent was still half sticking out. She turned to me, our eyes locked. I didn't look away, there was no reason to be embarrassed at being caught staring. It might be the last time I would be able to.

"Well, most people who were infected just concentrated on being shot in the head before they turned instead of— "

"Fuck you."

Delilah still looked furious and her ire only seemed to increase the longer I kept watching her. We hadn't had a civil conversation in months, the closest we got was whenever I helped fold her tent. I wished I could make it up to her somehow. I wished I could just apologise and have her forgive me and have everything be alright again, but it was too late for that.

"I'm sorry."

"No you're not."

The cold wind seemed to bite into the wound on my arm. While my arm felt completely numb, the wound never stopped burning, biting, throbbing. I could feel the infection flowing through my veins, numbing everything it touched. Gerald helped Delilah fold her tent properly. I silently thanked him. He'd done so much for me already, I couldn't ask him to take care of Delilah for me as well, but it seemed he had decided to do so all on his own.

"I am *sorry, I didn't mean— "*

"Have you given up on your ridiculous theory?"

"No."

"Then I can't forgive you."

No one liked my theory. They said it was disrespectful. I

disagreed, even though I could see where they were coming from. I wasn't trying to be disrespectful to the memory of the dead. It wasn't like I hadn't lost my own family to the plague as well. But that didn't change the fact that I fully believed, with all my heart, that with the right mindset, it was possible to not lose your mind.

Nearing footsteps brought me out of my thoughts. Everyone was packed up and ready. All the people I once called friends stood before me, towering over me from how I was sitting on the ground. The ground had stopped feeling cold a while ago.

Even though everyone was here, I only had eyes for Delilah and Gerald. Gerald, the one person who hadn't stopped being my friend even once I voiced my theory. Delilah, the person I missed the most when she stopped talking to me.

I would miss them, all of them, but mostly Delilah. Even when she was angry at me, at least she was always nearby for me to hear and see. Now she would leave me all alone.

I wondered if she would miss me as well.

"Rose..." she said, trailing off as if she wasn't sure what to say. Mixed emotions played on her face. There was the anger that was always there whenever she looked at or thought about me, but when she said my name... I was sure I heard sadness there. I didn't want Delilah to be sad, but it made me feel a little better to know that she wasn't happy about me dying.

She shook her head, clearing her expression of all emotion. "Good luck," she said, voice as cold as the wind still biting at my wound. She turned around, but I stopped her before she could take a step away from me.

"What about the ropes?" My voice was small, weak. The poison was so fast-acting. I could hardly feel anything anymore except for the pounding of my heart, the throbbing of my wounded arm.

Delilah froze in her tracks, then slowly turned to me. Her face was twisted in disdain. "We're already taking a risk by not shooting you in the head!" I flinched at the reminder. Delilah hadn't hesitated to make known what she wanted to do with me the moment she saw the deep scratches on my arm. "Be glad Gerald insisted on honouring your wishes." I glanced at Gerald for a moment, giving him a weak smile. He wiped at his eyes, before giving me a smile in return. I wished I could cheer him up somehow.

I shifted in my ropes, but none of the uncomfortable numbness went away. They were old ropes. They wouldn't use the best ones just to tie me up. I might be able to break out if I tried hard enough. Maybe I could bite through them?

Delilah was still glaring at me, but she didn't look angry anymore. She looked scared. "You're right, Delilah," I said. If I *did* turn and lose my mind, I wouldn't want to roam the woods and potentially kill and infect others. "I'm sorry."

Delilah nodded, her expression blank again. She turned her back to me, but she didn't walk. "Good luck," she said. This time the words came out unsteadily, chocked up. My breath hitched. I suddenly had the desperate urge to say something, anything, to make her stay, but no words would come out past the lump in my throat. Delilah moved, and the others followed. Their footsteps slowly faded into the distance, until only silence remained.

I was alone.

My vision wavered. I wasn't sure if it was from tears or the poison. It hurt. My heart beat wildly in my chest, erratic, struggling, and only pumping the infection further through my body. Had it reached my mind yet? Would I feel it happen? Or would I fall unconscious and wake up either with the proof my theory was correct, or as a mindless zombie?

Black spots clouded my sight, there was a rushing in my ears.

A foot landed in the corner of my vision, followed by another. And I realised the rushing in my ears wasn't the pumping of my blood, but the sound of hundreds of shuffling footsteps. The hoard had reached me.

I prepared to be jumped, to be clawed at and bitten and scratched. But...

But the first zombie passed me by. And then the second. They ignored me. I let out a rattling breath, and noticed for the first time that my breath *was* rattling.

I— had it happened? Did I do it?

My incredulous laugh came out wrong and wailing. The zombies turned their heads but then continued ignoring me.

I'd done it.

I continued to wail, this time less an attempt at a laugh and more in true despair. What the hell was I supposed to do now? I was alone, tied to a tree. I couldn't talk, couldn't even laugh. Saliva pooled in my mouth, hunger gnawed at my stomach. My fingers hurt under my nails, where I knew they'd soon begin to bleed. All the tools of the infection ready for spreading it to more people.

What use was my mind when I was still dead and alone?

A Face

A boy walked through a forest. His pink hair contrasted against the dark green of the plants. His steps were determined, confident. His shoes looked like new, even though he must have been walking for days now. Even his clothes still looked pristine. As if the soft flowing fabrics managed to dodge every hooked thorn, every grabbing branch. As if they flowed right through them.

Through the trees towering high above him, a light shone. His pace increased. Although the forest floor was covered in dry leaves and branches, he didn't make a sound as he walked. There was complete silence. Not a single bird sang in the darkness.

He stopped in front of a monstrous house. Towering pointed roofs, walls made of dark stone, dark windows. Enormous double doors like a giant mouth. Even here the trees didn't let any light through. Only one stained window was lit up. The doors opened for him as he approached.

He stepped into a hallway as dark and menacing as the outside of the house. Rotting wooden stairs sagged against stone walls, an emptiness pervaded like a physical presence, there in the undisturbed layer of dust. He climbed the old wooden stairs without a sound. At the top stood another door. Golden accents reflected the light coming from underneath. Muffled clinking of tableware broke the silence. The last step creaked. The door swung open without as much as a gesture.

He walked into a grand wide open hall with high ceilings, steps echoing on marble floors. The hall was bright, lit up brilliantly by a glittering chandelier hanging above a table that stretched the length of the hall. People sitting at the table raised their glasses to him. He didn't recognise them. They didn't have faces. He sat down at the head of the table and took a sip of wine. It was sweet. He paused, frowned. Something was wrong.

He scanned around the table, examining the faceless people one by one. He stopped. His eyes turned flinty. A face. A girl. Sitting right in between the faceless people. She studied him intently, bright eyes moved from his pink hair to his well-tailored clothes. He didn't have the patience to pull the same charade. "How did you get here?" he asked. His voice, while not loud, seemed to echo through the hall. The girl snapped out of her inspection, but didn't answer.

He put down his glass. Around the table, the faceless people continued their meal. "This," he said, leaning over the table, "is my dream." He loomed over her, lowered his voice to a deadly whisper. "I want to know what you're doing in *my* dream."

The girl didn't answer. Just kept watching him with wide-open eyes. He had her pinned down with his glare. She sat frozen, not even daring to breathe. His nostrils flared. He pushed himself up, snapped his fingers. The faceless people around the table, who up until now hadn't reacted to the commotion at all, turned their blank heads to him in unison. He gestured to the girl.

"Wake her up."

Agustin's Winter

When the Drowned Oracle confirmed the death of Captain Agustin, the winter ended. It had been a long one, characterised by bright sunlight refracting off snow and ice, cold and timeless. And while the end of winter was celebrated by all, there was also a sense of loss. For that winter was warmed by the flourishing light that was Agustin, and the captain was now lost.

Agustin was a prominent figure in the general Overijssel area. A poet and storyteller known all across the various cities and villages. With a sharp top hat, even sharper goatee and round gleaming glasses, Agustin cut a distinct figure. They were rather fluid about their form of address, often going by 'they', but sometimes going be 'he' as well. But at the end of the day, throughout the winter that would forever carry their name, they would prefer to be known simply as 'captain'.

That the winter would be long became apparent early on in November, when icy winds cut through the streets, snow lay thick on rooftops and shards of ice drifted along the river. It was probably the sight of that ice that led one old sailor to retire and put her old vessel up for sale.

It was a raggedy thing. A small steamer with room for no

more than ten. With peeling paint and rusty pipes not even hidden from sight, barnacles and fungus taking over the sides. They say Agustin took one look at it and bought the thing without even a cursory attempt at haggling.

No one knew quite what to make of it. Agustin had never shown an interest in the sea before, and when looking at them, they didn't seem the type. Always wearing a well-tailored trenchcoat and slacks, pointed shoes with a clicking step, and of course the before-mentioned top hat, they looked rather proper. Not like a sailor at all.

They were the type for slow walks in the city. Parties and dinners in polite company. Evenings in well-maintained bars where they told their stories to captivated audiences. They were not the type of person to set off to sea in a ragged little boat filled with burly sailors.

When asked, Agustin would smile politely, and give an infuriatingly vague answer that didn't explain anything at all. Most people decided they were looking for inspiration for a new story. More likely though, the reason was simpler. The same reason so many others drop their livelihoods to do seemingly nonsensical things;

The calling.

It can happen to anyone. Be it a calling to the sea, like with Agustin, or a call to go live in the forest filled with dangerous creatures, or to check out the lighthouse that's said to be haunted. It lights up the mind, brightens the eyes until they almost glow with it. Parents live in fear of seeing that light in their children's eyes. For no matter what they do, no matter the horrifying warning tales they tell, there's no stopping someone with a calling. They move with a purpose only they understand, a purpose that can't be swayed. And that was certainly true for Agustin.

Soon after buying the ship, Agustin went in search of crew. By all rights, this should have been difficult. Some wannabe high-society poet who'd never before set foot on a ship calling themselves captain and thinking experienced sailors would listen to them? Who'd put their lives in the hands of someone like that?

But Agustin had charisma in spades, as anyone who ever met them could tell you. Sailors flocked to them, almost begging for a spot on their ship, and it definitely wasn't because of the offered gold. Agustin just had this air about them. The same air that drew in invitations to fancy parties, allowed them unquestioned access to restricted areas, and led people to tell them their deepest secrets.

It was this same air that led to Agustin and crew's triumphant return, just two weeks after leaving for their first voyage.

Now what success meant exactly to Agustin and their crew, no one knew. The ship wasn't big enough to be a proper merchant, and they weren't working for the navy either as far as anyone knew. Freelance captaining? Is that a thing? If anyone could do it, it would surely be Agustin.

If anyone had paid attention to a certain shadowed corner, they might have noticed the man listening to their whispered conversations with a smirk. Had the gossipers recognised this man as Admiral Kennedy, then maybe they would have revised their opinion. Agustin might not be working for the navy, but that didn't mean the captain couldn't be compensated for any information they might glean in foreign ports.

Agustin's charm didn't end with the people of the Netherlands. No, foreigners were just as taken with them as everyone else. And so just like back home, Agustin schmoozed themselves into parties and dinners, and left with a stomach filled with food, and a mind filled with secrets.

Agustin's return was celebrated with boisterous nights in town, everyone welcome to join in. It soon became tradition, every time the captain was home.

On those nights, Agustin regaled captivated audiences

with tales of foreign ports, clandestine meetings and invitations to secret clubs.

One time, they proudly recounted their victory over a pirate vessel. An exciting if standard tale of cannons, pistols and various near-misses. It's only after the action was over, when the story seemed to end, that Agustin's eyes really lit up with excitement. They let the attention of the audience wane for just a moment, letting them believe it was over, but then raised their voice to continue.

Long after the other ship vanished under the waves, when they were already turned around to continue their journey, the crew called out, "A survivor!" Someone was still clinging to floating debris. Agustin smiled as the audience hushed in anticipation, letting tension build as they described their hauling the person up the side of the ship. The only survivor, drenched in saltwater, defenceless and completely at their mercy. And who would it be that they rescued, but the pirate captain herself!

The audience gasped, what did Agustin do then? Throw her back overboard? Lock her up to face justice once they returned home?

"Alas," Agustin said, "she was too fast." They held out their arm, rolling up the sleeve to reveal a deep gash, halfway healed. The pirate captain was a fearsome warrior who had used her hidden blade to attack before they realised. She'd run away to the emergency rowboat and used it to escape.

A curious ending to such a triumphant tale, isn't it? You'd think they'd embellish a little, maybe lie and say Agustin won the battle on deck, killing the pirate captain heroically and getting wounded in the process. It would have made them look better to the audience. A proper tale of victory.

But as Agustin later regaled to the admiral they were getting increasingly close to; the ending was *already* a lie. Once they dragged the captain aboard, she didn't attack at all. No, Agustin actually handed her some supplies and led her to the rowboat, letting her go off to find a new ship to captain.

The wound on Agustin's arm came from a sailor who didn't agree with letting murderous pirates free without facing justice. Said sailor was regrettably killed in the scuffle that resulted from the pirate captain's escape, according to the official story at least.

So yeah, for once, Agustin chose a lie that would make them look a bit stupid, because they couldn't exactly admit to helping a pirate without getting in trouble themselves. But why then, were they so excited to tell that particular part of the tale? They could have left out the surviving captain entirely, after all.

Well, Agustin was a poet at heart. This tale wasn't yet complete. That night, they were laying the groundwork for a more epic story later on. For what was a more compelling story than that of a captain and their *rival*?

Subsequent returns to town were from then on often accompanied by more tales of run-ins with the same pirate. Tales that of course ended with her getting away once again.

And afterwards, the captain would retreat to the darker recesses of the bar and listen to the stories of others. Other captains, sailors, poets, writers and braggarts. And it's there in those quiet corners they met with Admiral Kennedy again and again.

Himself a prominent figure around port, there were many rumours about the man. Some said he was a spy, others that he ran shady business under the table, still others believed him the only non-corrupt political figure. None of them were entirely right.

Kennedy wasn't a spy for anyone but himself and the navy. He wasn't a perfectly innocent angel either, since he'd be forced to arrest Agustin if that were the case. Shady business? Well, paying Agustin for information could be seen as shady. Accurate rumours or not, there was something remarkable about the admiral. Where for years people had been drawn in by Agustin, it seemed they'd finally found someone who drew them in turn.

That first night they were seen leaving the bar *together,* eyes only for each other, chaos reined behind them.

When Agustin left port once more, the engine glowed even brighter, resonating with their happiness. Agustin and their ship's radiance cut through winter as not even the sun could.

With a few successful voyages now under their belt, it seemed nothing could go wrong for Agustin. That, of course, couldn't be further from the truth. Agustin's inexperience at seafaring had to surface at some point. And it wasn't in their lack of knowledge of steam engines, or in managing the crew, or in finances that honestly shouldn't be as favourable as they were. No, in this case Agustin's downfall came from the small fact that not all sailors' superstitions were well known to land-dwellers as Agustin had been not even three months before.

One cold day in February, when the sun glinted harsh of the ice-covered deck, so bright its heat wobbled the air, a cry sounded from the deck. A sailor, a young lad barely old enough to work, was in hysterics. "It's watching me! It follows..."

He pointed to a big white bird perched on the railing. Piercing grey eyes, rimmed by blue, were indeed locked on the poor young sailor. Agustin had never seen such a bird before. Its beak, blue-grey in colour, had black streaks running from back to front, like it'd once shattered and was then glued together again.

As it lifted its beak to the sky to let out a guttural cry, the eyes remained focused on the sailor, peeking out from either side of the beak. From above, an answering cry sounded.

There, hovering on the wind, were more of them, only these didn't seem interested in the crew. They hovered on strong wings, more arm like than of a regular bird, stiff and tipped with black feathers like gloves. Birds of Wake, the sailors called them.

Agustin looked at the bird on the railing, its head tilted downwards once more. A bird of Wake... They knew of Wake of course. The force that destabilises reality, drives people mad, makes them vanish.

But never before had they heard of a bird of Wake.

"A Jan Van Gent," a sailor whispered in their ear, "a Gannet. They come from the other world. Wake sends them, to watch, to warn..."

Agustin was a poet, a storyteller. Their whole life had been spent both listening to the stories of others and telling their own. If they were an expert at anything, it was in this. They knew exactly how to make people believe, how to start rumours, weave fantastic imaginings together with truth until they couldn't be told apart.

In the case of Wake, most stories could be taken with a grain of salt. And so despite never having heard of the birds of Wake before, Agustin thought they could see where reality and fiction ended.

They dismissed the warning with a careless wave of the hand. All that mattered in that moment was that this bird was upsetting one of their sailors. As captain, it was their duty to make any danger, perceived or real, go away.

They drew their gun, took aim.

The crew looked on, petrified.

The bullet sailed, hit the bird right in the chest.

For a moment, all went still. Then red bloomed on the white feathers, piercing grey eyes switched to Agustin before turning glassy, and the bird toppled over the railing to fall limp into the sea.

Satisfied, Agustin holstered their gun and looked back to the previously upset sailor to give him a pat on the shoulder and send him back to work. But then they noticed the silence, the tension. The young sailor was pale, still shaking, and wouldn't look in Agustin's direction. The other sailors as well looked away. Unnerved, but also irritated, the captain retreated to their quarters.

Wake, the god of endings. The power that makes people vanish, erases minds. Loss without the opportunity for goodbyes. To be cursed by Wake is not nothing. That night as they fell asleep, all Agustin saw behind their eyelids was the momentary reflection of a top hat in glassy eyes.

While the crew would talk to Agustin as normal and the ship remained on course back home just fine, no one would look them in the eye. When they arrived at port, Agustin was the first to leave the ship, completely done with the tension that had loomed the whole way back. They couldn't wait to warm themselves at the bar where everyone would treat them like usual. Maybe the admiral would stop by as well.

Just half a step off the plank, they were stopped by the harbourmaster, a spark of something in her eyes that set Agustin even more on edge.

"A message for you, Captain."

They took it, opened it. The letter slipped from shaking hands, landing on the docks where moisture soaked into the paper. The harbourmaster picked it back up before the words turned illegible, pressed it back into Agustin's hands all while patting their shoulder consolingly. As the water-blotched message declared, the admiral was gone. Agustin would never see their love again, no one would.

Wake is the god of loss. Before you scorn Wake, think of all you could lose to its curse.

Agustin had learned their lesson.

Without the warmth of their lover, or at the very least the knowledge their lover was waiting for them somewhere out there, Agustin went cold. The following days and weeks the winter picked up a notch. Agustin's melancholy permeated the entire ship. The engine struggled to stay alight and the crew had to sleep in piles around the fire to stay warm.

Without the admiral, Agustin had no one to sell information to, and what was previously a successful voyage to celebrate, was now a futile endeavour that quickly dried out the small bit of gold they'd saved. The crates of fuel and food they could afford became smaller and smaller, until the rations weren't enough to stave off the constant hunger, until the engines fire slunk ever smaller.

Before, Agustin might have saved them by talking to rich benefactors or charming free meals for the crew from kindly restaurant owners, but now it just didn't work. Their grief was still too raw. The happy person people flocked to was lost under a veil of gloom.

Two sailors left the ship one day at port and never returned, taking their chances elsewhere. The remaining crew gathered and whispered while Agustin slept. They were sick of this, it couldn't go on like this. If the captain didn't get a decent meal together for them within the next week, they'd take matters into their own hands.

And sure enough, a week later Agustin was cornered on the ice-covered deck. Four of their burliest sailors had the captain surrounded, their faces contorted in anger. For the first time in weeks, Agustin snapped out of the haze they'd been living in and properly took in their surroundings. Beyond the four in front of them stood the others, looking less angry, a little more hesitant, but not stopping their fellows either.

Despite the anger directed at them, Agustin couldn't find it within themselves to feel threatened. Strong as the sailors were, they all looked exhausted. Eyes bruised from bad nights, clothes loose from lack of food, anger barely covering desperation and fear.

All Agustin could think in that moment, was that this was all their fault. They had to fix this, somehow. Deep in the heart of the ship, the engine sparked a bit brighter.

But then the sailor in front of them talked, and Agustin went cold. "We're taking over the ship." No, that wasn't right. They couldn't take the ship. The ship was all they had left. No house, no money, no admiral. But the ship was still there, still keeping them moving despite the fact they hadn't had enough fuel to stoke a proper fire in days.

They looked around at the crew, four standing ready for battle, another watching their backs. Three others standing unsure, not really agreeing but not standing up for Agustin either.

Agustin could have given up, maybe they should have. The numbers weren't in their favour. But Agustin was just as desperate, had been driven mad just like the rest of them. And those words, that declaration, sparked a depth of feeling that'd been missing since the Admiral vanished. Rage twisted Agustin's features, and before anyone knew what happened the captain's gun was drawn and smoking, and the first sailor lay bleeding on deck.

The battle that followed was violent and brutal. Warm blood hissed as it hit the frozen deck. Blades clanged together and gunshots echoed in the still air.

Then finally, it was over, and Agustin stood victorious over the bodies of their mutinous crew. Battered but alive, three sailors stood with them. The engineer—a mysterious woman whose words always held a double meaning—, the young sailor for whom Agustin angered Wake, and a strong woman who was once a soldier.

Four people weren't enough to properly keep the ship running though. They set course back home, but the going was slow. While the engine kept warmer than it had in the last weeks, the lack of fuel set an agonising pace. They didn't say it, but they all knew they'd run out of food before they ever made it home. Still reeling from the violence they couldn't scrub off their minds or the frozen deck and without hope for the future, it was no surprise they were quietly driven ever closer to madness.

The last day of winter arrived at the beginning of April. It was a bright noon, the sun so violent and present it warmed right through the winter chill. The light rippled the world, warping reality until they were never sure what they were seeing and what they weren't. It's in this state they were besieged by pirates.

The pirates took them by surprise, the rippling air having hidden their vessel from sight. But even if they'd spotted them earlier, they never stood a chance. Four wounded against a full crew of bloodthirsty pirates.

The young sailor was so frightened by the sight he was taken by Wake right then and there, vanished before their eyes. Maybe his fate was preferable to death by pirates or drowning.

Canons fired into the defenceless ship. One shattering through the hull and hitting the engine full on. With the death of its heart, the ship swayed one last time—

—and sunk beneath the waves, just five short months, one long winter, after Agustin first left port.

It's said that the remaining crew survived though. Agustin might have been gone, but their legacy survived. And just as Agustin had once fished a pirate captain out of the sea only to let them go free, now the very same pirate captain picked up the two women clinging to the floating debris.

Further Credit

Original prompt for the story 'Mind Reading' by Reddit user u/Cuckmandu

> *Everyone in the world has the ability read minds, except for you. It is treated as such a normal and inconsequential fact of life that it is rarely if ever brought up. Because of this, you have no knowledge of this world of mind readers.*

Original prompt for the story 'Captured Calamity' by Reddit user u/Xedro

> *Bad things always happen to people you photograph. You're torn between treating this as a curse or exploiting it as a gift.*

Original prompt for the story 'That Coat' by Reddit user u/ItsHeredditary

> *You're walking alone down a dark road one night when you see a stranger coming towards you. Give the stranger one unusual piece of attire, one mannerism, and one line of dialogue to make the encounter as creepy and unsettling as possible without being overtly or explicitly sinister.*

Original prompt for the story 'Wandering Spirit' by Reddit user u/The_OG_upgoatMost

> *Ghosts are bound to certain locations, but not this wandering spirit.*

Original prompts for the story 'The 13th Hour' by Reddit

user u/aglet_factorial

> *This guy is going places. Not old age. But places.*
>
> *The kind of guy who will sweep you off your feet and then drop you on your head.*
>
> *Poor impulse control and a can-do attitude are a dangerous combination.*

And by Reddit user u/oceanicscribbles

> *The clocktower struck the 13th hour.*

Inspiration for the story 'Outstandingly Fine' was a Tumblr post by user vampireapologist

> *I have 15 years' worth of outstanding library fines in three separate cities and it's my hope that eventually a bounty hunter librarian will come to collect them and we'll get in a bar fight and fall in love.*

Inspiration for the story 'Love is the voice over the shady companies intercom' was a Tumblr post by user foulserpent

> *I think my ideal job is being paid 50$/hour to sit on the computer doing whatever I want at an empty rented office space for mysterious employers definitely running some kind of money laundering scheme and just needing me to keep up appearances of one of their shell companies but I'm not like, in on anything and no one can charge me for anything.*

Thank You

Thank you for reading my first ever book!

If you enjoyed my stories, then please consider leaving a review. If you did not enjoy them... well I'd rather you not leave a negative review, to be honest. Haha.

This collection contained some of my favourite stories, but they're by no means my only ones. If you want to read more, head over to my website!

www.robinegberts.com

And maybe subscribe to my email list so you won't miss any new releases!

Thanks again! I love you!

About The Author

Hi, I'm Robin Egberts and I write short stories and sometimes even some longer stories. About magic, horror, dreams and the unimaginable vastness of space.

I started writing these short stories to practice keeping my ideas concise, because my novel length projects kept getting longer each draft. But I very quickly found a love for writing these shorter stories.

Sometimes I tailor a story to practice a specific element of writing, like dialogue or description. And other times it's to experiment with an idea or a narrative voice I haven't tried before. Most of the time I just have an idea for fun plot or character and want to share it.

Besides writing and reading, I also enjoy taking pictures of mushrooms, building terrariums filled with all kinds of insects, cuddling with my cats, getting lost in the peaceful environment of my aquarium, taking walks in nature, drawing, playing video games, playing minuet in G on my keyboard, and just hanging out in my plant-filled bedroom.

www.ingramcontent.com/pod-product-compliance
Lightning Source LLC
LaVergne TN
LVHW090932150826
845672LV00006B/1481

* 9 7 8 9 0 8 3 2 6 8 6 0 6 *